John Stilwell Applegate

Reminiscences and letters of George Arrowsmith of New Jersey

John Stilwell Applegate

Reminiscences and letters of George Arrowsmith of New Jersey

ISBN/EAN: 9783337147396

Printed in Europe, USA, Canada, Australia, Japan

Cover: Foto ©Andreas Hilbeck / pixelio.de

More available books at **www.hansebooks.com**

REMINISCENCES AND LETTERS OF
GEORGE ARROWSMITH.

Yours truly,
George Arrowsmith

REMINISCENCES AND LETTERS

OF

GEORGE ARROWSMITH

OF NEW JERSEY

LATE LIEUTENANT-COLONEL OF THE ONE HUNDRED
AND FIFTY-SEVENTH REGIMENT, NEW YORK
STATE VOLUNTEERS

BY

JOHN S. APPLEGATE

RED BANK, N. J.
JOHN H. COOK, PUBLISHER
1893

PRESS OF THE REGISTER,
RED BANK, N. J.

TO

ARROWSMITH POST,

NO. 61, DEPARTMENT OF NEW JERSEY, GRAND

ARMY OF THE REPUBLIC, THIS BOOK IS

RESPECTFULLY DEDICATED.

NOTE.

The immediate occasion of the preparation of this work was the acceptance of an invitation to address Arrowsmith Post of the Grand Army of the Republic upon the subject of "George Arrowsmith." The task was a pleasant one, as I was only discharging a debt due to the memory of my friend. Owing to the fact that his military service had been rendered among the troops of other States, the Post knew little of his history, further than that he was a native of this vicinity, a sterling patriot and a gallant soldier. I sought, therefore, to produce a record as complete as it was possible to do with sources of information limited by the lapse of time. The

work grew insensibly on my hands, beyond the
limits of an ordinary discourse, and in a form
materially abridged I presented it to the Post
at a public meeting held under its auspices on
the evening of Decoration Day, 1891. Now, at
the request of a number of those who were endeared to the soldier for his many excellent
qualities, and of others, who, though personally
unacquainted with him, are interested in his
history as members of the organization that
bears his name, I have undertaken to publish
the matter I have collected, intending it as a
simple memorial of a brave and loyal man.

J. S. A.

Red Bank, N. J., December 7th, 1893.

CONTENTS.

LIEUTENANT-COLONEL ARROWSMITH.

INTRODUCTORY.

THERE are many heroes in American history who have won national fame. There are many others whose reputations are more circumscribed, but who were just as brave, just as patriotic, just as self-sacrificing. The last may be counted by the hundreds of thousands who, at the call of the President for volunteers, went forth from the counting-house, the farm, the workshop to engage in deadly strife with the enemies of our country. Many were young men of rare promise, talented, cultured and brave, and who might have attained high national distinction in civil or military life, but were cut down in battle at the very threshold of their career. As observed by President Lincoln in a compliment to the character and intelligence of regiments arriving in Washington at the beginning of the civil war, they contained individuals quite competent to discharge the functions of the highest executive office of the nation.

I propose to speak of one of these gallant heroes, a youth of brilliant promise, cut down in the morning of life; a soldier of this republic, who entered the field to die, if need be, for the honor of its flag, with no expectation of a return to peaceful pursuits until the object of the war had been accomplished.

ANCESTORS.

GEORGE ARROWSMITH was born on the eighteenth day of April, 1839, in the part of Middletown township (now Holmdel) near Harmony meeting-house. He was a descendant of a family of Arrowsmiths, settled on Staten Island about the year 1683, who were Englishmen, occupying a prominent position in society, and had rendered public service, both of a military and judicial character. His father was Thomas Arrowsmith, a farmer by occupation, who owned a farm on which he resided, and a mill, at what was then known as Arrowsmith's Mills. He was a man of limited educational advantages, but naturally gifted with superior mental endowments. His manner was mild and his disposition social. He had stored his mind with the information of general reading, and

thus with the advantage of a retentive memory,
was an instructive and entertaining conversation-
alist, as well as a pleasing public speaker. His
simplicity of character was such that even beyond middle life he found pleasure in the company of boys in their teens, and. there are those
living who, when boys, have spent a pleasant
hour in his society and profited by his counsel.
He was quite an effective public speaker. In
my early law practice I crossed swords with him
on one occasion before a road tribunal, when he
spoke in his own behalf, and I found him by
reason of the high respect he commanded as a
citizen, supplemented by his persuasive diction
and adroit manner of presenting his case, a
dangerous adversary In the village debating
society—and the village debating society was
no small factor in our civilization fifty years ago
—his varied information usually enabled him to
bear the palm.   He enjoyed in a high degree
the confidence of his fellow citizens.   He was a
veteran of the war of 1812 and a major in the
State militia.   For a number of years he served
the Township of Middletown as its assessor of
taxes.   In 1835 he was elected a member of the
legislative counsel of New Jersey, a position cor-
responding with that of State Senator under the
constitution of 1844.   In this capacity he served
two years, being succeeded by the late Hon.

William L. Dayton. In 1843 he was elected to
the responsible position of Treasurer of the
State of New Jersey, holding the office until
1845. From 1848 until 1850 he was a member
of the board of Chosen Freeholders for the
township of Raritan, being the first to represent
that township on the Board. From February,
1852, until February, 1858, he was one of the lay
judges of the Court of Errors and Appeals of
New Jersey. In all these official positions he
discharged his duties creditably and acceptably
to the public, and his integrity was never as-
sailed. He died December 27th, 1866, at the
age of seventy-two years. The loss of his son
was a crushing grief, and like Jacob when he
refused to be comforted and said "I will go
down unto the grave unto my son mourning,"
his death followed swiftly. The mother of
George was Emma VanBrackle, a lady of quiet
manner, but whose countenance seemed radiant
with maternal tenderness and affection, and
whose life was "full of good works and alms
deeds which she did." She was a daughter of
Hon. Matthias VanBrackle of Monmouth county,
a substantial farmer who in 1820 represented his
district in the State legislature. She survived
the death of her husband a few years.

There were born to Thomas and Emma Arrowsmith nine children. Joseph Edgar Arrow-

smith, long well known as a leading physician
of the county, resident at Keyport ; John V. Arrowsmith, a highly respected citizen, also resident at Keyport ; Eleanor, the esteemed wife of
Daniel Roberts ; Cordelia, a lovely young lady,
who died at the early age of twenty years ;
Thomas Arrowsmith, who in the beginning of
the civil war enlisted in the Eighth Pennsylvania
cavalry, and was subsequently promoted to the
position of Brigade Quartermaster with the rank
of Major, serving until the end of the war, and
who afterwards engaged in teaching; Stephen,
who died in infancy; Emma, a much beloved
sister, who is lately deceased; George, the subject of this sketch; and Stephen V. Arrowsmith,
the present principal of the Keyport graded
school, where he has successfully served the public for fifteen years.

EARLY LIFE.

A T the old Harmony school house in the vicinity of his home George obtained his preliminary educational training. Here he was intimately associated as a fellow pupil with Major Charles B. Parsons, who was destined to become a fellow soldier in the army of the Union, and a commander of the Grand Army Post bearing his playmate's name. I first met George as a schoolmate at the Middletown Academy about the year 1851. Among others in our class were Thomas Field, now deceased, a young man of much promise; the Rev. Thomas Hanlon, D. D., President of Pennington Seminary; the Hon. George C. Beekman, late presiding judge of the Court of Common Pleas and State Senator; and Jacob T. Stout, the enterprising contractor of Atlantic Highlands. At

this early age George manifested a military taste.
Even at a much younger period, as his mother
used to say, "he was completely carried away
with anything that pertained to soldiers." A
pack of schoolboys trooping as wild horses
would suggest to his mind a charging squadron
of cavalry; and later, upon the college hill, on a
quiet Sabbath morn, listening to peals of the
church bells in the valley below, he would recall
Napoleon's fondness for such an incident. Head-
ley's "Washington and his Generals" and "Napoleon and his Marshals," were favorite books.
His admiration for the fighting qualities and
dash of Marshals Ney and Murat and Benedict
Arnold was unbounded, though bitter in his denunciation of Arnold's treason. His first composition at the Middletown Academy was upon
the subject of George Washington. It made a
lasting impression on my mind as a bright production by so young an author. Throughout
his academic course all his orations and essays,
so far as I can remember, were upon historical
subjects or characters. In school he was bright
and tractable. Out of school he was a leader in
sport and never offensive to his play fellows.
Once I saw him angry. An older boy stood before him, vexing him with gibes and raillery. He
stood like a statue, silent and sullen, but occasionally expressing defiance by throwing a key

which hung suspended by a string around his neck towards his tormentor's face. It was not difficult for his assailant to interpret the action, and he wisely suspended his offensive conduct.

"The charm of his character," said Dr. Lockwood in an obituary address, "was his filial obedience. It was a volume of eulogy condensed into one heart utterance, when the aged father said to me in words almost choked by the sense of his bereavement, 'George was a good boy; I never once had occasion to chastise him.'"

After a short attendance at school at Middletown Point, he entered the grammar school connected with Madison University at Hamilton, New York, in May, 1854. I was already a student there, and being old schoolmates, we took a room together in No. 31, first floor, Western Edifice, at the southwesterly entrance. It was by far the noisiest room on the Hill, and we made it noisier by unmelodious practising upon violins, evoking emphatic protests from our neighbors, who I fear have never entirely forgiven us for the many joyless hours we caused them.

In housekeeping we suffered no adversity worse than a holiday spent in exasperating efforts to put up and connect a line of disjointed stove pipe. I might add for the benefit of the

curious reader that there were no expressions
of a profane nature accompanying the work,
though what we said internally—well, that is
not legal evidence.

On another occasion our domestic bliss was
marred by bitterness and disappointment. We
bought some pretty paper to decorate the walls
of our room. To save expense we put it on
ourselves. It was not artistically done, but it
was better than bare walls. As the paper became thoroughly dried, we observed that whenever a fire was started and the room warmed
up a crackling sound would be heard around the
borders. Investigation showed it was the paper
gradually loosening day by day, greatly disturb-
ing the equanimity of our tempers, until finally
it was indeed a sorry spectacle, hanging upon
the wall in rolls and festoons. But there was
a lesson derived from the experience, which is
never to paper a whitewashed wall.

COLLEGE DAYS.

IN October, 1855, George entered the Fresh-
man class of Madison University at the age
of sixteen. He was allotted to the Æonian
Society, one of the two literary societies then
existing in the college. Though the youngest
student, he took and maintained a high rank
both in class and in literary work. He could
acquire with little effort and was a sprightly
and ready writer. Socially he was highly esteemed, and was a general favorite with students
and townspeople. While his face was not of
the handsome type, yet he passed as a handsome man. Height, five feet, eleven inches, hair
black and long, complexion dark, dark hazel
eyes, a face serious in repose, form erect and
spare, weight one hundred and forty pounds,
and a manly bearing, all combined to produce

a military figure that would be noticed in a crowd.

He was popular with the ladies and fond of ladies' society, though I never knew of his being especially devoted to any one, beyond what was consistent with a mere friendly partiality. I recall a query propounded by a young lady student at the Hamilton Female Seminary in the reading of her paper at a public meeting of its literary society, "Does Arrowsmith manufacture Cupid's arrows?"

He was possessed of superior musical gifts. Throughout his academic course he sang in the college choir and glee club. Having a deep and melodious bass voice, it was rarely indeed that he was not one of a musical party that afforded pleasant entertainment in a serenade or at an evening concert. He also excelled in instrumental music as an amateur performer upon the piano, organ, bass viol and violin. In college sports he was never a laggard, though not an athlete. In his day, athletics were not a college specialty as now, and in the absence of practice there was little opportunity for development in that line. He was fond of swimming, skating and coasting. I recall an incident when on a Thanksgiving Day a party of which he was one skated down the Chenango canal to Earlville and back, a distance of twelve miles. The last one to arrive at Earlville was to pay for the oysters for the party. The last was a Virginian, who enlisted in the war on the Confederate side, and was killed in battle at the explosion of the mine before Petersburg.

A coasting incident I have not forgotten. Mounting the same sled, we started for breakfast to the boarding hall, quarter of a mile away. With polished runners, a steep descent and smooth ice, we shot down the ravine like an arrow. It was impossible to round that curve without upsetting, so we headed straight down a sloping field. Half way across, with unslackened speed, we struck a ditch concealed under the snow. There followed an exhibition of stars, infinite in variety, succeeded by a tableau, suggestive of the "wreck of matter and the crush of worlds."

In college pranks George was a good follower, but never a leader. And even as a follower he recognized the limits of self-respect. If a proposed scheme involved an element of dishonor, his ready answer was "No, that will be mean;" but an innocent affair like "ringing the rust" or a "mock scheme" for a Junior Exhibition or a Young American Celebration of the Fourth of July, he entered into with ardor.

An incident will illustrate the harmless character of his college jokes. When the first submarine Atlantic cable was laid and messages of congratulation had passed between the President and the Queen, there was a sudden interruption of communication. While the people were eagerly waiting for the next message, which owing to an accident was delayed, George overnight printed some placards (he had learned to set type in the village printing office) and posted them around town, greeting the public eye the next morning with the following announcement: "Latest by submarine cable! The Duke of Cambridge's cows broke into the Queen's garden last night and destroyed her cabbages." For about two hours those in the secret enjoyed the spectacle of people gathered in knots about the streets, discussing the latest intelligence from Europe, and the great wonders the magnetic telegraph had wrought.

True to his ancestry, George was a staunch Democrat in politics, and though educated in a rank Republican town, his political faith was unshaken by his environment. His political activities began at the age of seventeen, when he made himself quite popular with his party in Hamilton as a stump speaker for Buchanan and Breckenridge. The success of the Democracy in that campaign was the occasion of a Democratic festival in celebration of the victory, given at the Eagle Hotel at Hamilton, on which occasion

Arrowsmith was called out and made a speech which was received with great favor and specially complimented in the next issue of the *Democratic Union.* About this time a letter written to his brother Stephen indicates his lively interest in the political campaign. "Everything reminds me of the old times in Trenton (he lived in Trenton, N. J., while his father was State Treasurer from 1843 to 1845) when I used to get 'licked' so by the Whig boys of Mr. Minses's school. There is a Buchanan club in the village and I frequently go to their room to read the papers; but I wish you would send me the *Washington Union* every week. That will be easier than to write a letter and I will take it as a propitious omen that you are all well. It will be quite a curiosity here where abolitionism and black republicanism run rampant." In the same year, 1856, George was an occasional writer for the newspapers of his own county. In the issue of the *New Jersey Standard* of May 1st, 1856, there appears an article written by him entitled "Cromwell and Bonaparte," and signed "Scriptor." It evidences the remarkable maturity of his intellect at the period of his seventeenth birthday.

In the Æonian Literary Society George took a high rank as a writer and orator, and all its principal honors were bestowed upon him. He

filled successively the offices of Critic, Vice President and President. At its public meeting in
his senior year he delivered the valedictory oration. The following complimentary notice of
one of his orations before a public meeting of
the society appeared in the *Hamilton Republican*:
  " The next oration, Subject : ' Excess of Political Freedom,' reflected high honor upon the
genius of its composer. In the production of
this speech, Mr. Arrowsmith not only honored
himself with the reputation of one of the best
writers in the University, but manifested ability
as an orator that will confidently defy competi-
tion. The grace of his style, the easy flow of
his expressive diction, the palmy fulness of his
periods, combined with the spicy, piquant
quaintness of humor that so appropriately and
unostensibly insinuated itself in the composition,
lent a telling effect to his effort. Mr. Arrowsmith is destined to leave his own mark on the
political future of his country."
  It used to be a custom in Hamilton for the
youths of the village to celebrate the Fourth of
July by a ceremony distinctively Young American. After a parade on horseback by a hundred
or more young men fantastically dressed and
masked, they would draw up in the park
around a platform to listen to speeches. Among
the pleasant reminiscences of my college life

was an occasion in 1857 when George was a
participant in a celebration of this character and
one of the orators of the day. His personality
disguised, his argument was in keeping with his
appearance, very grotesque.   Referring to the
question of prohibition, he suggested three
methods of reform.   The first, which he thought
would be popular with the reformers, was for
they themselves to drink up all the liquor, so
that none would be left for the anti-reformers.
The second was to petition the legislature to
pass a law forbidding the use of intoxicating
beverages by every citizen, excepting members
of the legislature.   Such a bill, he thought
would be popular with the members of the
legislature and sure to pass.   The third was a
gradual reduction of the strength of liquors by
dilution with water until it came to be adminis-
tered in such homœopathic doses that it could
do no mischief.   The last was sure to be popular
with the whiskey venders.   The question of
slavery, then the exciting topic of the country,
also received his attention.   "Are we all," he
said, " to be made nigger slaves to the South ?
Is that old monster slavery to rear its black and
grizzly form over the fair North and vomit up
pollution over the verdant hills and people of
New York? No! Let us rather say in the language of the immortal Webster in reply to De-

mosthenes—Liberty and Death—Henry Ward
Beecher forever—Sharp's rifles, inevitable and
let her burn—I repeat it, sir—let her burn.
Fellow citizens, my feelings overcome me when
I touch upon such a subject. When I see republicanism trodden under foot and scorned—
the pathfinder of freedom and salt river defeated
in a National election, I am prompted to seize
the American Eagle by the tail feathers and
twist him round the head of the Government
until by the flapping of his wings there is not a
quill left large enough to make a pen for a
pettifogging lawyer."

There is more, but this will do to show that
as a boy of eighteen, he was not a sleepy one.

The Mu chapter of the Delta Kappa Epsilon
Fraternity of Madison University was organized
in 1856. Arrowsmith was one of its founders.
It had existed hardly two years when the faculty
determined to uproot it, upon the ground that
the existence of a Greek letter society in the
college was inimical to its prosperity. About
one-half of its members promptly yielded to the
pressure of the faculty and withdrew from the
society. The remainder by standing firmer
succeeded in effecting a compromise and saving
the chapter. Arrowsmith was one of the latter.
His loyalty to the fraternity was intense. He
clung to its memory while he lived and died in

battle wearing its emblem near his heart. It may be of interest to add that the Delta Kappa Epsilon Fraternity is no longer proscribed at Madison (now Colgate), but flourishes with the favor of the college authorities. *Tempora mutantur*, etc.

In his Junior year he became a subject of the Divine grace and united with the Hamilton Baptist Church. He had always yielded a reverential attention to religious matters. Before his conversion he would welcome to his room the class prayer meeting, and would open the exercises by reading a chapter from the Bible. "The fact of his conversion," said Dr. Lockwood at his funeral, "he communicated to his parents in a way so joyous and artless as showed that he had become really a child of the Kingdom of God. As near as I can remember his words addressed first to his mother are: 'Dear Mother, I am going to bed, but first I must sit down to write you some good news. I trust I have found the Saviour. O, what a change! Dear Father, I feel now that I have a great Friend above who will help me to carry out your good advice to me.'" Fully three years afterward in a letter addressed to his brother, referring to the conversion of the latter, "Be assured," he says, "that the intelligence was very gratifying to me. One thing is certain, you have

never done a nobler or more important thing in
your life than that which you mention, transact-
ing business for eternity. Your determination
has greatly pleased me as it will all your *true*
friends. Your step, as you say, ought not to
deprive you of any real pleasure. Who in the
world has more reason to be happy than he who
has a friend in the all-powerful and ever-present
Being who rules the world? The Christian is
the only person in the world who may be said
really to fear nothing."

In the year 1858, after the destruction by in-
cendiaries of the Quarantine Hospital on Staten
Island, there was a strong public sentiment
manifested by the New York press in favor of
reëstablishing the hospital on the Jersey shore at
Sandy Hook. This stirred up an indignant opposition in New Jersey, and especially in Monmouth County, whose rich and fertile lands and
prosperous summer resorts would be seriously
prejudiced by the location of a pest-house upon
its shores. George's pen was active in denunciation of the scheme, furnishing articles which appeared in the *New York Times* and the *Trenton
True American*. These articles were copied and
circulated widely throughout the State and were
regarded with much favor as a clear and effective
presentation of the case from New Jersey's
standpoint.

George was graduated in the class of 1859 at the age of twenty years. The *Republican* in its account of the Commencement exercises thus commented upon his Commencement oration:

" Mr. George Arrowsmith was the next speaker and with the deliberation and ease seldom observable on Commencement occasions, proceeded to discuss in eloquent and perspicuous language, the popular subject, ' National Institutions.' For racy and unique style, terse and vigorous thought, and finish of illustration, this oration was a superior production, and Mr. Arrowsmith's effort was a triumphant one, excelled by none of the day, and won for him many laurels, as well as a shower of bouquets thrown to him on retiring from the stage."

Among his classmates whom I now recall were Hon. Enos Clarke, Henry A. Cordo, D.D., Wayland Hoyt, D.D., Hon. William A. Lewis, Egbert R. Middlebrook, Esq., Daniel E. Pope, Esq., Thomas Edgar Stillman, Esq., and George M. Stone, D.D.

LAW STUDENT AND TUTOR

DURING his college life he was frequently disturbed by the thought that he was enjoying comparatively an easy life, spending the money which his brother and father at home were working hard to earn; and in letters to his brother he referred to it occasionally, expressing a wish that he too could be making a living. He intended at the close of his collegiate course to study law. This he saw would involve further expense to his father. Moved by these considerations, he conceived the idea of teaching in Hamilton, in conjunction with the pursuit of his legal studies. Accordingly, on June 19th, 1859, he wrote his father from Hamilton that the position of tutor in the Grammar School had been tendered him by an almost unanimous vote of the faculty, announcing his disposition to

accept it and his reasons, and asking his father's
views and advice upon the subject. P. P.
Brown, Jr., the principal of the Grammar School
connected with the University, a warm friend,
wrote to his father about the same time stating:
"It gives me great pleasure to announce to you
that the faculty of the University with great
cordiality, unanimously voted to-day to recom-
mend your son George to the board of the University, to be appointed assistant teacher in the
Grammar School, commencing in October with
the next academic year. The different members
of the faculty expressed themselves as highly
pleased with his scholarship and manly deportment and had no doubt of his success in his new
position."

George accepted the position tendered him and
in October, 1859, entered upon his duties. At
the same time he entered the law office of Hon.
Charles Mason, a Judge of the Supreme Court,
and the leading lawyer of Madison County,
under whose direction he pursued his legal
studies. Thus is explained how he came to
study law and afterwards to be admitted to the
bar in New York rather than in New Jersey,
the State of his nativity, where his success could
have been promoted by the aid of influential
relatives and friends. It was a matter of convenience rather than choice, for he was a Jersey-

man at heart, though he had formed many strong friendships and pleasant associations in the place of his adopted home. Two years later in a letter addressed to the writer, who was then a law student in Trenton, New Jersey, after expressing regrets that he too could not be studying in the same State, he says, "but my divinity that shapes my end has seemed to decree otherwise ;" and again he says in the same letter, "I do wish I could come to Trenton, and if it were not for losing all I have done in this State I should think about it."

For three or four years before his enlistment he was a frequent contributor to the *Union*, a Democratic paper of Hamilton, furnishing many spicy and incisive articles of a partisan nature. This led to a personal difficulty in March, 1860, with the editor of the opposition paper, who was Thomas L. James, afterwards Postmaster of New York, and later Postmaster-General in the cabinet of President Garfield. Malevolence, however, could find no place in the heart of either. Forgiveness quickly interceded and amicable relations were restored.

About the year 1860 or '61, a road controversy occurred between George's father, Major Arrowsmith, and some of his neighbors, in which an altercation arose between George and Henry S. Little, Esq., the lawyer for the applicants. It has been reported that George on this occasion actually assaulted Mr. Little, which is not true. As the affair excited much interest, and erroneous impressions still prevail as to how far George lost the control of his temper on this occasion, Senator Little at my request furnished me with an account of it as follows :

"Your request for information in regard to the road case in which George Arrowsmith and I had some altercation is before me. So many incidents had escaped me that I delayed answering you until I could see Senator Hendrickson, who was one of my clients in the matter. Yesterday I dined with him and refreshed my memory by his. He and the Major were close friends, politically and otherwise. In this case they were wide apart, as were many farmers on the line of the new road. The road ended in the Middletown and Keyport road, I believe, near the mill, and was the continuation of a road that extended up through the Senator's property, and enabled the farmers in that section to go down to the shore for fish and other purposes, and went shy of the Major's mill. He opposed it with his accustomed skill and, as you know, was a most formidable adversary. At that time road cases were fought under a black flag, no quarter being given or asked. The Major had many roads that converged to his mill—this one did not; and posted by the Senator and others, I made a hot fight, doubtless said things exasperating enough to stir as cool a man as the Major, and more than enough to anger his young and gallant son. We must have had a good case for the surveyors laid the road. This finally maddened George and he violently denounced me, and probably but for the interference of his friends would have assaulted me. I never blamed him; on the contrary, respected him all the more for defending his old father. I have no doubt I was in fault for not using more moderation. After there was time for cooling we were just as good friends as before. That was saying not a little, for I was a warm admirer of his. His patriotism had stood as mine had against adverse surrounding influences. You may remember the peace meeting that well nigh led to bloodshed at Middletown. Most of the Democrats of influence had signed a call for a meeting to denounce the administration and declare for peace. I refused to sign it and so far as it could be done was read out of the party. So you see there was a bond of union between us. I do not know after writing so much that I have aided you in the slightest to anything that may be useful."

Senator Little, holding the affirmative of the

case, had the right of reply. As he says, he
doubtless said things exasperating enough—a
statement no one will controvert who is at all
familiar with Mr. Little's sarcasm and the freedom with which he was wont to use it. When
he had finished, George arose to reply. Mr. Little objected. This application of the "gag law,"
as George considered it, is probably what stirred
his anger more than anything else, and led to
the violent denunciation of his opponent. As
his most intimate friends know, George was
possessed of a tranquil demeanor not easily disturbed. The circumstances mentioned only
show that he could be aggressively impetuous
for cause. It was not a weakness. On the battle field a like impetuosity of temperament won
for him the appellation of the " Young Lion."

Senator Little's reference to the famous or in-
famous Middletown peace meeting recalls vivid-
ly the distinction between the two kinds of
Democrats of those times. One carried the flag
and kept step to the music of the Union. The
other was quite indifferent to both flag and
Union, and loyal only to party. George was of
the former class, as subsequent pages will illustrate.

HIS PATRIOTISM KINDLED.

I N April, 1861, George passed his legal examination and was duly licensed as a member of the New York bar. About this time occurred the assault on Fort Sumter. Excited crowds of citizens nightly gathered around the village post-office, impatiently awaiting the distribution of the mails with the latest news from Charleston Harbor. On one of these occasions a rebel sympathizer, hearing the announcement that the National flag was actually assaulted, suffered his enthusiasm to elope with his judgment by an open avowal of a wish that the South might succeed, adding that he for one was ready to fight with them. George was present, and instantly mounting a box, called for the man who had uttered the treasonable sentiment, demanding a retraction. A retraction not forthcoming,

he denounced him as a vile traitor in terms of
bitter wrath and indignation until the man
quailed under his fiery invective and slunk out
of view. "No man," he said, "could insult the
national emblem in his presence without his indignant protest." His patriotism kindling as
he proceeded, he proclaimed he was willing
then and there to enlist as a soldier in the Union
cause, and appealing to the crowd he asked,
"How many will go with me?" There were
numerous responses. In a few hours fifty men
had signed the muster-roll. On Monday, April
29th, these assembled at their rendezvous, and
organizing under the name of the Union
Guards, unanimously selected George Arrowsmith as their Captain. The *Republican* of Hamilton, in a magnanimous spirit, forgetting past
differences, commended the selection in the following generous terms of approval : "The ex-
cellence of the selection is not to be disputed.
Captain Arrowsmith is a young man of high
character and fine abilities. He will be every
inch a soldier, as he is a scholar, and if the opportunity offers, the Hamilton Volunteers under
his lead will attain all the honor and glory to
which, we are led to believe, their aspirations
reach."

They prepared at once for their departure to
Utica to join Colonel Christian's regiment, then

forming. It was a solemn day for Hamilton.
Business was entirely suspended. The weather
was delightful, and the village was thronged
with people. There were many aching hearts
and tearful eyes. Fifty of the noblest, bravest
and best young men of Hamilton leaving their
homes and kindred to confront the dangers of
war ! At eleven o'clock the procession formed
under the direction of three leading citizens of
the town, acting as Marshals. These were
Lieutenant Colonel H. G. Beardsley, Senator
John J. Foote and James Putman. The order
was as follows : First, Band ; second, Volunteers, under command of Captain George Arrowsmith ; third, Clergy and Professors of Madison
University; fourth, Ladies ; fifth, Citizens.
After parading the principal streets, they assembled in front of the hotel, where a fervent and
affecting prayer was offered by the Rev. W. A.
Brooks, after which, on behalf of the ladies of
Hamilton, David J. Mitchell, Esq , an eminent
lawyer then of Syracuse, but formerly of Hamilton, who had done great service by his war
speeches in arousing the public enthusiasm, presented the company with a beautiful silk banner
in a stirring and eloquent speech, which was responded to by Captain Arrowsmith with due
acknowledgments for himself and company.
After a presentation to Captain Arrowsmith of

an elegant revolver and a like presentation to
two other officers, by different citizens, the volunteers entered vehicles, and "amidst a perfect
tempest of cheers and waving of handkerchiefs,"
started for Utica. The report of the occasion
says there were uttered many a "God speed
you," and many a tear trickled down the cheeks
of those who had loved ones among the patriots,
as they moved away.

ENROLLMENT AS A SOLDIER.

THE journey of twenty-nine miles was a series of ovations. Arriving at Utica they were quartered in the City Hall, where they partook of a supper provided for them. The next morning they were sworn in, and being now enrolled, they proceeded to the election of officers, George Arrowsmith being chosen Captain as at the informal election of the day before. The company was soon filled up to the requisite number of men and joined the Twenty-sixth Regiment, New York Volunteers, recruited in the vicinity of Utica, and received the designation of Company D. The regiment proceeded to the military post at Elmira, where it remained two months in barracks, and improved its time in drilling and parading.

Shortly after the arrival of the regiment at

Elmira, Captain Arrowsmith addressed the ladies of Hamilton the following letter, acknowledging in grateful terms the receipt of their gifts, consisting of four barrels of numerous luxuries in the form of eatables and clothing :

ELMIRA, N. Y., May 17th, 1861.

To the Ladies of Hamilton :

Your gift was received yesterday, and received with a good round of cheers, I assure you. Just previous to their arrival, we received the kind letter which you sent us, and I read it to the company assembled around the stove in the rough barracks, eager to hear anything from those at home whose sympathy they are confident of participating in.

In three or four instances since we left Hamilton, have we found it necessary to throw to the breeze the beautiful banner which you presented us, to keep the company together. Your letter, followed so closely by *four* barrels full of solid " sympathy," will do more to keep the peace and preserve order for three or four days, than so many barrels of " army regulations " would. The butter and shirts were acceptable especially. " The rations " do not include butter, and the latter on account of the delay of the military departments in getting our uniforms, were absolutely indispensable. The cakes are considered to be luxuries which are not to be lightly spoken of by anybody. But we value the moral influence of your gift still more highly than its tangible effects.

Immediately after your letter was read and duly " cheered and tigered " (by the way, the cakes have since been " tigered," though they were cheered on their arrival) I was deputized to write a letter thanking the ladies of Hamilton, on the part of the company. By this imperfect note I have endeavored to comply with their request, at the same time feeling as I write, exceedingly thankful, for a certain large cake which has been received, and solemnly disposed of by the captain of the aforesaid company.

Ladies of Hamilton, accept our thanks. You will not be forgotten by us, and we hope still in the future to occupy a niche in your memory.

GEORGE ARROWSMITH,
In behalf of Company D.

Afterwards the Hamilton ladies formed themselves into an organization for the purpose of providing comforts for the volunteers enlisted from their village and the vicinity.*

Before leaving for the war, Dr. Eaton, the

---

*Appendix, Note B.

President of Madison University, wrote and gave to George the following letter of commendation which he no doubt thought might serve him usefully in the South, where the doctor had many acquaintances, in the event of his capture by the enemy. It was like Dr. Eaton, whose heart was always full of kind promptings, to be thus thoughtful :

MADISON UNIVERSITY, April 24, 1861.

The bearer, *Mr. George Arrowsmith*, graduated from Madison University in the class of '59, and discharged the office of tutor during the following year, as an assistant to Professor Brown, Principal of the Grammar School of the University.

Mr. Arrowsmith held a high rank in his class as a young gentleman of marked ability, fine scholarship and correct deportment. He discharged the duties of tutor in a manner highly satisfactory to the faculty and to the students who enjoyed his instructions. It is therefore, but simple justice to Mr. Arrowsmith to commend him, as I do, most cordially to the respect and confidence of the wise and good everywhere and to the public generally.

GEORGE W. EATON,
President of Madison University.

Captain Arrowsmith found his duties as commandant too engrossing to afford time to correspond with all his friends individually, and to make one letter answer for many he sent a communication to the Utica *Herald* from time to time over the signature of Aliquis. These letters are interesting as a part of the history of his regiment and of his army life. Under date of June 9th, 1861, he writes from the Elmira Barracks as follows :

ELMIRA, BARRACKS No. 3, June 9, 1861.
To the Editor of the Utica Morning Herald:

Since my last letter the regiment has been unusually busy in drilling and parading, and also unusually zealous in view of so on being ordered off. On Thursday afternoon we received intelligence that a party of Uticans, with the colors, were on their way to Elmira. This was very welcome news, I assure you. On Friday morning squads of men from the companies scattered in all directions to bring in evergreens and bouquets to decorate the barracks, in which work there was quite a spirit of emulation. In an hour or two the appearance of the camp was wonderfully changed. Rows of cedar trees suddenly appeared before the barracks, the flag-staffs ornamented with wreaths and bouquets,

and all sorts of mottoes and decorations were
fixed on the neighboring buildings—some of the
men solemnly declared "it was a regular Fourth
of July." At eleven o'clock the regiment was
drawn into line for the presentation of colors,
which were soon exposed to view amid a murmur of admiration. Judge Smith, of Oneida
County, made the presentation speech, which
was characterized by his usual ability and vi-
vacity. It was heard in silence by the immense
crowd of spectators who on foot and in carriages
were pressing around the lines. Colonel Christian received the colors before the regiment, and
replied with military brevity—the few words
with which he intrusted to them that flag will
not soon be forgotten by the regiment. A very
large crowd of citizens, townsmen and towns-
women, as I before said, witnessed the presentation of the flag, and the troops were gratified to
notice that the Female College for the first time
had come in procession upon its grounds to witness the parade.

The colors were presented by Mr. William H.
Lewis of your city, whose arrival in town was
a source of great joy among his numerous
friends in the regiment. Mr. Lewis and Judge
Smith have been "lionized" among the men
ever since the ceremony. After the presentation the whole regiment marched to the resi-

dence of Mrs. Maxwell, at whose commodious
mansion the Colonel has his rooms, and the
colors were there left while the procession
returned. I cannot, by the way, mention the
name of Mrs. Maxwell without also mention-
ing that she has proved herself, ever since
we have been here, a true friend to the regiment, and never has the private or officer
been turned from her door when she could furnish anything to supply his wants or suit his
convenience.

On Friday afternoon also we received our ac-
coutrements, canteens, knapsacks, haversacks,
belts, ammunition boxes, tents, camp kettles,
which gave the camp an appearance still more
military—but still no caps or underclothes !
What culpable delay ! The day closed with a
parade down through the town accompanied by
our Utica friends.

There never has been a better feeling in the
regiment since its stay at Elmira than there is
at present. There is a crowd of spectators
every afternoon to witness our battalion drills—
this afternoon several hundred. Our Utica
friends, ladies and all, have been on the grounds
a great part of the time since they arrived,
and yesterday Mr. Long got them up a dinner for all in the officers' mess room. I took
a little pains to notice the kind of fare which

he provided, and found it as follows: Beef soup, roast beef, boiled beef, mashed potatoes, pickled tongue, rice pudding, French "co-quettes," with tea and the usual fixings. Mr. Long did not at all give them an opportunity to test "the hardships of camp life."

To-morrow morning we suppose most of our guests will start for Utica.

Still waiting for orders! ALIQUIS.

Before the Twenty-sixth Regiment had left Elmira, Arrowsmith acquired an enviable repu-tation as an officer. A visitor to the camp writes under date of June 11th, 1861, that he found Captain Arrowsmith and his Company pleasantly situated. "The Captain," he states, "is highly spoken of by his fellow-officers, and is an especial favorite of those in superior com-mand. His company is looking as well and is under as good drill as any in the regiment. Colonel Christian says there is no better officer in the regiment."

The day before leaving Elmira for Washing-ton George writes as follows:

ELMIRA, BARRACKS No. 3, June 19, 1861.
To the Editor of the Utica Morning Herald:

I trust I am now writing my last letter from Elmira. It is stale news to you, probably, th a

last Friday it was announced by the Colonel
that we were to march to Washington yesterday. Those who were sick at heart from "hope
long deferred," suddenly brightened up, but
those who had the measles and mumps, and
such unromantic and unwarlike diseases, did
not recover so easily. So for this reason, and
because we would have to go in freight cars on
Tuesday, we deferred our departure until next
Friday.

When the above announcement was made to
the regiment in line, there followed the wildest
and most picturesque scene that I ever witnessed. As if in accordance with a premeditat-
ed plan, the men immediately hung their caps
on their bayonets and broke into companies,
which marched around the grounds in all directions, amid the wildest screaming and huzzas.
This intelligence has also had the effect to sepa-
rate the chaff from the wheat, and there have
been some, but very few, desertions. Many
have absented themselves from duty, but have
returned after seeing their friends, or transact-
ing such important business as visiting wives,
etc. Last Sunday night the men were unusually
uneasy, and just before dark fourteen of them,
with their side arms, ran the guard at once, and
were pursued by several of the picket guard.
After dark the report came to the camp that

they were pursued by the guard in a large wood, but refused to be taken. The Colonel immediately despatched a captain and twenty men to bring them in, who duly tore their clothes, tumbled over rocks, and fell in the mud in the search, with military promptness, but in vain. When the captain wished to collect them to return home, several shots were fired as signals, which had the effect to bring out the surgeons toward the forest with the grim prospect of having some fine subjects. Such are some of the incidents of the camp. The fourteen delinquents, however, have all been taken or have returned.

For the last week the regiment has used as a drilling ground a large field above the barracks, where there is ample space for all battalion movements, and I assure you drilling has been carried on as much as the physical powers of soldiers could sanction. The men take an especial interest in street firing, with a view to Baltimore, I expect, for it is now well settled that we are to start on Friday morning, with three days' provisions and fifteen thousand rounds of cartridges. Our caps and shoes are now all provided, and the former make a great improvement in the appearance of the regiment. To-night they made a second parade down the town and were lustily applauded by the other regiments as they passed their barracks. One

of the evening papers in town contains the following paragraph :

" This afternoon Colonel Christian, of the
Twenty-sixth Regiment, was unexpectedly presented with a splendid charger by Mr. W. H.
Lewis, on the part of the citizens of Utica. The
presentation was made suddenly and with but
little ceremony, but the soldiers gave three hearty
cheers as the Colonel mounted the horse and rode
along the lines. A good present well bestowed."

Both officers and men in this regiment feel
very grateful to the ladies of Utica and vicinity
for the interest they have taken in our welfare,
displayed as it has been, in the liberal donations
which we have received. You cannot imagine
the moral effect, aside from the substantial benefit, of the boxes of clothing which your Utica
ladies have from time to time sent to us. Imposed upon by clothing contractors, and really
neglected by the State government, our pay
delayed on account of Albany technicalities,
these donations have often revived the droop-
ing spirits of the men—the mere idea that some
one was interested in them. The ladies of Utica
will long be remembered with pleasure by the
Twenty-sixth Regiment.

To-morrow we are ordered to pack up and
have everything in readiness to move.

ALIQUIS.

EN ROUTE FOR WASHINGTON.

O N Thursday, June 20th, the regiment started for Washington. The following letter
is descriptive of the trip:

MERIDIAN HEIGHTS, WASHINGTON, {
June 27th, 1861. {

To the Editor of the Utica Morning Herald:

Excuse my tardiness in writing, but the confusion consequent upon our moving from Elmira and the inconveniences of camp life have
hitherto discouraged me. However, I have now
reconciled myself to circumstances, and am sitting on the ground, writing on a box of cartridges with a dull lead pencil.

Our trip from Elmira was very pleasant in
the main, though as we got more and more
toward the South we began to find some pretty

warm weather. We started with nineteen cars
and two locomotives, and did not change trains
until we arrived at Baltimore. At Williamsport
the regiment received a fine ovation, were paraded through the streets, entertained by the
ladies in the finest picnic style—that reminded us
all of the old Sabbath-school celebrations ere
our country had let slip the dogs of war—every
man received a cigar after the collation, and
amid loud cheering the heavy train bearing the
regiment slowly moved from the town. It appeared as though every inhabitant in the town
was down at the depot to see us off, and thus all
along the road did the best of feeling seem to
be manifested towards the volunteers. We rode
all night, made no stop at Harrisburg, and in
the gray of the morning passed a guide board
with "The State Line" upon it. Then did your
correspondent cautiously protrude his head
from the car window, realizing that he was now
" down South "—saw no vile secessionist aiming
at it—became very bold and cried "hurrah !"—
saw no man that looked like Jefferson Davis's
portrait, so I did not fire my musket; pickets
all along the road to Baltimore, encamped
along beautiful streams, guarding the bridges
and whiling away the long summer days in
shooting at a target.

The scenery along the road from Harrisburg

to Baltimore is very picturesque, and the trip
was thus rendered quite pleasant and interesting. No secession flags were seen, but we were
greeted with Union demonstrations as we passed
along. Finally we arrive at Baltimore, after
loading at the last station. There are crowds
of people along the streets, but with the exception of a few dubious remarks and hisses, there
are no symptoms of disturbance. The troops
march through in grim silence, replying to no
question, and not allowed to receive refresh-
ments or water from the crowd, though in the
broiling sun. Two or three that drank water
proffered by men in the crowd were afterwards
very sick and afflicted with sore mouths, and
it is thought their abstaining from Baltimore
water was very fortunate. The inhabitants that
followed us to the depot, however, seemed to be
all true to the Union. Our stay in Baltimore
was very short, for the Washington train started
as soon as the regiment got on board. We arrived in Washington, having passed on our way
several camps and the celebrated Relay House.

By the time we arrived at the station near the
Capitol, we were considerably worn out, having
had little or no sleep in the cars the night before, and having exhausted most of the two
days' provisions which we took from Elmira.
The men now saw their error in packing so

many articles in their knapsacks, for I assure
you every pound counted in the oppressive heat
and the broiling sun of Washington.   On alight-
ing from the train we found we had to march to
Meridian Heights, a hill about three miles from
the city.   Some of the men fainted and fell out
on the march up, overcome with heat and fatigue, but the men from the camps which we
passed on the way up encouraged the boys,
helped them carry their muskets and baggage,
and in various ways expressed the sympathy of
brother soldiers.   The men have recovered from
this fatigue, and are healthier on the whole than
they were in Elmira.   The night we arrived our
tents had to be erected, and as it was getting
late, many slept in the open air—but we were
sufficiently fatigued to sleep almost anywhere.

Our ground, called Camp VanValkenburgh, is
finely suited for parading purposes, but is badly
supplied with water.   All the wells around here
which we use are constantly guarded, as some
have been poisoned by the Virginians.

We are now drawing our rations, but in the
confusion attendant upon getting this military
machinery fairly at work we frequently take
some long fasts, just long enough to make us
relish the pork, bread and coffee when we get
it.   We are, however, getting along better and
better every day.

In our tents we of course sleep generally on the "ground floor," with knapsacks, valises or stumps for pillows, and happy are they who have waterproof blankets to lie upon. Our tents are rather scarce and rather small, and not infrequently we see feet and legs protruding from under the canvas, which, in case of a shower are vigorously hauled in. In lack of the usual conveniences, bayonets serve for forks and candlesticks, brush houses for kitchens, have-locks for handkerchiefs, ammunition boxes for seats and tables ; while at times there are vague rumors that shoes and boots will have to be used to make soup and jerked beef of. It is a novel life, but we have every confidence that our Quartermaster will make it as agreeable as pos-sible.

Our captains are to-day engaged in making out our new pay rolls, and we understand that they will be immediately responded to. We are also encouraged to hear that we are sure to be newly uniformed and armed in a few days.

We have been alarmed and under arms twice already. Last Friday night a sentinel of the Thirty-eighth, New York Volunteers, fired his piece, and ten of our regiments were instantly drawn in line of battle. A company of flying artillery also started from the city. Last night, also, some cannonading along the river occa-

sioned a "long roll" in all quarters, and all the
regiments in the vicinity were under arms. In
neither case was there any occasion for the
alarm, but scouting parties of the federal regiments frequently run into the pickets of their
own friends and occasion a general alarm, but
nevertheless we are obliged to hold ourselves in
readiness for action. Right on our flank lies
the Thirty-eighth; in a field about two hundred yards from us lies the Eighteenth, and just
beyond them in a large grove is the Fourteenth,
and a number of other New York regiments
scattered all around in the vicinity.

I cannot, like a regular Washington correspondent, tell all about the strange sights, for
I've had no chance to see anything but the outside of the Capitol as yet—at present I'd like to
see a good, comfortable hotel.

ALIQUIS.

Occasionally Captain Arrowsmith found opportunity to run up to the city of Washington.
The capital was a new place to him and he saw
much to interest him, especially in the way of
politicians and other celebrities. "Here," says
Eli Perkins, "he made my room his headquarters where on my return I frequently found
him installed with a bevy of officers. You know
George did love a good story with a fine point.

How he used to read Artemus Ward to me !"
On his return from Washington he writes his
brother under date of July 8th, 1861:

"In the reading rooms of Willard's Hotel I find
a great deal to interest me. I saw there last
night J. C. Breckenridge, N. P. Willis, Secretary
Cameron, Thurlow Weed, Colonel Bartlett,
Donnelly, of Wise-Donnelly letter notoriety,
and in fact army and naval officers, politicians
and congressmen by the hundred. * * * *
We are sworn in the United States service only
till the twenty-first of August, when I suppose
we will return home. I have learned considerable of military service, and if I ever go into it
again, I shall strike for a field office. I suppose
I might get a lieutenancy in the regular army,
which I would like first rate. I am going to look
around a little with a view to that while I am
here."

He writes of a want of tent accommodations,
there being but one tent for five persons, and
proceeds: "We sleep on the ground with waterproof blankets under us to keep off the damp-
ness. These were given to our company by the
Hamilton ladies, who have an organized society
to attend to our wants. Our victuals consist of
pork, bacon, beef, coffee, beans, rice and bread,
which are weighed out, so much to each man.
This is cooked and eaten in the open air. The

men cook their own food in little frames, with
seven iron kettles and stew pans. We get plenty
to eat, 'such as it is, and it is good enough what
there is of it.' Once when I first arrived I went
twenty-four hours without eating anything, but
it was more to keep the men from complaining
than because I could not get it, for the officers
can generally get along pretty well. There is
always more or less confusion when we move
from one place to another, and sometimes lack of
provisions, but usually there is plenty. I stand
it very well now, never was hardier, and have
learned to eat pork and drink raw coffee. The
men do their washing in a beautiful stream near
the camp, in which they go in squads. My
waiter does mine, of course, the whole object
being merely to get them clean, starching and
ironing being out of the question. We have two
battalion drills every day, one in the morning
and the other in the evening. Sometimes the
whole regiment fires ball cartridges at once in
the side of a hill by way of exercise. The
muskets carry ounce balls about the size of a
common marble, which trim the limbs from the
trees in front of us finely, I assure you. Some
of the farmers around are Union men, and some
secessionists, but the latter are compelled to
keep very quiet. We are very careful as to the
politics of the pedlars of whom we buy eatables.

One of my company was poisoned coming
through Baltimore, and hasn't been well since.
The country looks just like Jersey in nearly
every respect, and the days are not much warmer
than a good hot Jersey day."

BATTLE OF BULL RUN.

O N SUNDAY, July 21st, the Twenty-sixth Regiment left Washington about noon and marched to Alexandria, where it arrived about two o'clock. Here it waited until night for a train to transport it to Bull Run, where the battle was going on. July 23d Aliquis writes from Shooter's Hill, near Alexandria, Virginia, as follows:

SHOOTER'S HILL, VA., July 23, 1861.
To the Editor of the Utica Morning Herald:

Still another step towards a battle and still a more lively realization of real soldiering. We left Washington on Sunday about noon, leaving the sick to guard our camp, and arrived at Alexandria about two o'clock, where we had to wait a great while to get a train which could transport us to the scene of action whither we were marching.   Alexandria is indeed a desolate town.   Grass grows in the streets, business appears suspended, men look dismal and unhappy, and everything reminds of war.   The Marshal House is continually crowded with soldiers tearing up staircases, floors, etc., to get pieces of wood with Ellsworth's blood on, which, by the way, must have flowed in great abundance in the young man's veins, if I may judge from the numerous specimens I have seen.   While waiting at Alexandria, we continually heard heavy cannonading from the south, but night came on, and we finally lay down to sleep in a field near the depot, in the open air.   Soon, however, we were called up and put on a train, the tops and platforms crowded wherever a man could stick on, and we started towards Fairfax.   Aliquis lay on top of a car, next to the locomotive, gravely winking occasionally, as the cinders flew in his eyes, and now and then "dreaming the happy hours away," when the train suddenly stopped at a station just this side of Fairfax, called Springfield.   There a picket was thrown out ahead, and we were stopped a while, during which we received the astounding intelligence that our forces were signally defeated, and we were ordered to fall back immediately to Alexandria.   When we got back we found Colonel

Kerrigan's regiment in the field which we had occupied, so we took an adjoining one and slept till morning, notwithstanding it had now begun to rain. When we awoke, trains crowded with retreating troops were coming hurriedly in, and the roads were crowded with stragglers from all sorts of regiments, in a weary and disorderly retreat. Our regiment now commenced its march up towards Fort Ellsworth, to cover their retreat so that they might rally behind us. And here a grotesque but most disheartening scene met our eyes—men from New Jersey, New York, Pennsylvania, Maine, all mixed up together, foot-sore and ragged, in no order, and apparently under no officers. All parts of the North were represented in the rout—Zouaves, with their gay uniforms torn, dirty and blood-soiled, soldiers without shoes, some without guns or knapsacks ; others, more determined, carrying away three or four of each ; some without eyes, some without ears and others with various flesh wounds, riding, limping or running—such was the picturesque procession which went along the road all yesterday forenoon. As they met us, they told us of the deadly fire of the batteries, told us to turn around immediately, and of the manner in which the rebels bayoneted all our wounded on the field, and such not very encour-ging details. Others cheered us, and hoped "we'd give 'em Jesse," etc. We finally went to Fort Ellsworth and entered it, where we thought the cannon, the abatis, the ditch and the ramparts looked very welcome after the accounts given us. Well, as the Dutchman said, we did not stop there, but went over beyond and bivouacked in a grove, where in a cold rain, without tents, we made sort of a cold breakfast. We expected an attack all day yesterday, and it was all we could do to keep the muskets dry. About noon the companies began to go off in search of better quarters. Aliquis and his company got into a deserted dwelling house, where with good fire-places and fences we managed to get comfortably dry. We put on extra pickets in the night, as it was reported that an immense force was approaching, and there is some danger of being pushed off into the Potomac. I really think the rebel General is very foolish if he does not attack us to-day. Most of our regiments are completely demoralized, and are crossing the river in crowds. The New York Twenty-sixth, Seventeenth, and some others, I think, are entitled to great credit for their present stand, as the majority are completely panic stricken. A Pennsylvania regiment near us is to-day hurriedly packing up to return home, their time having expired, which is not extremely encouraging either. The storm has now ceased, and

the morning is beautiful. Our ideas of the
enemy are all conjectural, and we know not
what to-day will bring forth. I hope, however,
when I write again to give you better news.

Among the consoling features of our soldiering is the good feeling among our troops. The
Captain of Company D was lately presented
with an elegant sword, a portable camp bed, a
camp stool, and other articles, by the members
of his company.   ALIQUIS.

The discouraging effect of the battle of Bull
Run upon our troops and their want of con-
dence in the ability of their commanders is reflected in the following letter :

SHOOTER'S HILL, VA., July 23, noon, 1861.
To the Editor of the Utica Morning Herald:

In my last I gave you our impressions of our
present state, as we had them this morning.
Now our situation seems no better, and our
regiment must shift for themselves. General
McDowell we know nothing of ; some say he yet
has a force with him to the south of us, others
that he is now at Arlington House completely
helpless ; others that he is in Washington. One
thing is certain : the few troops this side of the
river have no head that amounts to anything,
and rely solely on our Colonel Christian. There

are only about 4,000 men that can be relied on
this side of the Potomac. We are on the outposts,
along the Leesburg and Fairfax turnpikes, about
eight miles from the " Long Bridge " to Washington. We are hourly expecting an attack, in
which we shall hold out as long as we can, and
if compelled to retreat will fall back to the Long
Bridge. If unable to cross that, we will there
make a desperate stand on the banks of the river.
I have no confidence in any General or Colonel
near here but Christian. He yesterday recommended the occupying of certain hills near here,
which has been done. As it is now, we have to
rely upon ourselves, and we only hope our
Colonel may be made a Brigadier-General, as
is much talked of, and then we might indeed
be more secure. Regiments are continually
crossing to Washington, instead of crossing
from there here as it should be. I can count
from my present position three or four camps
entirely deserted. We have a Captain detailed
every day to command the pickets, which are
scouring the woods two or three miles towards
Fairfax.

The *New York Herald's* account of the battle
is a most egregious burlesque. If his reporter
had seen the disorderly rout that I have, he
would not have made so glaring a heading to
his column. Part of the regiments that he men-

tions were not at all in the action any more than
we were. As for us, we were ordered there and
then ordered back after the rout had begun.
There is nothing to hinder 15,000 rebels from
encamping right opposite Washington this morning, and we understand they have 170,000 between here and Richmond. As I said before,
there are only five or six regiments here that are
reliable—the others are breaking up and scatter-
ing, some to their homes, and some to Washington. I hope General Scott will soon restore
order, for in him we have all confidence, and
also in our Colonel ; beyond that deponent saith
nothing. We are to-day occupying some of the
camps that have been, as I should think, basely
deserted; but their tents are very acceptable.

ALIQUIS.

July 24, 1861.—Still there is no further advance of either army. There was no disturbance
last night, though we were called out once into
line by a "long roll" in some of the regiments
on our left. Yesterday afternoon scouts were sent
out around to ascertain our true state. Our regiment daily sends about fifty men some distance
up the Fairfax road as a picket, and yesterday
afternoon the Thirty-second New York Regiment came up and encamped just in the rear of
them. Near a Theological Seminary, on our

right, is the Fifteenth, under McLeod Murphy.
In Fort Ellsworth, which is about a quarter of a
mile from us, is Colonel Lansing with his Seventeenth, and also with a Massachusetts regiment
near him. Some others are also down on the
flats, but a great many of the camps there are
deserted. Last evening in the moonlight, the
woods in which we at first stopped, were entirely
cut down by our regiment, so as to expose the
Leesburg road to the guns of Fort Ellsworth.
Colonel Lansing also tore down a cemetery wall
near the fort, so as to use his guns to the best
advantage. Major Jennings, who had been sent
off by the Colonel on extra duty, returned
yesterday afternoon. We find, by the way, that
they have not forgotten us over in Washington.
About four o'clock yesterday afternoon we saw
a body of cavalry come up the road escorting a
carriage containing four persons—President
Lincoln, William H. Seward, General McDowell,
and our Adjutant, David Smith. The latter escorted them to Colonel Christian's headquarters,
where they remained for some time.

Colonel Christian occupies a large brick house
owned by a Major Smoot, now a Confederate
Major. Company B also is quartered in a portion of it. Company A is in a house near our
bivouac ground ; Company D in a large frame
house off on the right ; Company G in a house

on the left, used for a hospital ; the other companies occupy tents which were deserted by a
Pennsylvania regiment. It is on a beautiful
bluff where we are encamped, with a fine view
of the Potomac, while Washington with its large
buildings presents a splendid appearance in the
distance.

The defeat of McDowell is now known to be
much less than was at first supposed. Stragglers
are coming in even yet, and I suppose the regiments are speedily re-organizing over the river.
I can see this morning the glitter of bayonets
down along this side of the Potomac, as if a
regiment was moving from the Long Bridge to
Alexandria. I suppose a large army will soon
be gathered here again.

No more at present. I am now about to start
with a picket guard up the Fairfax road to
Clouds Mills. The officers and men are all out
watching a balloon, which has just gone up
from Washington.   ALIQUIS.

CAMP AND PICKET.

UNDER date of July 26th, 1861, Captain Arrowsmith writes his brother from Shooter's Hill, Va., a letter which indicates a better
feeling and a return of confidence among the
troops :

Dear Brother:

I have with my regiment crossed over into
Virginia. As you said in a letter (which I received last night) that you received the Utica
Herald regularly, there's no need of writing such
minute details in my letters home. We are still
quartered on Shooter's Hill, mostly in tents, but
I marched my company into an unoccupied
dwelling house, owned by a man now in the
rebel army. It is a fine, large house, and its
fireplaces and cupboards come very handily for
our use. We sleep around on the floors in all

sorts of positions. Half the houses around here have been thus deserted.

The first day or so after the battle this regiment was in a "ticklish" situation. The time of many regiments had expired and they hurriedly crossed the river, while others, panic stricken, followed them in a disorderly manner, leaving their tents still standing. It was generally believed that a large force of rebels were approaching. At one time there were only about four thousand left here. Now, however, they are returning—a large force is collecting—batteries are being erected—groves and forests are cut down to give free scope to the cannon, and desolation as usual betokens the presence of a large army. Last Wednesday the Colonel sent me off with a company of thirty-two picked men as a picket guard about five miles towards Fairfax, for the purpose of first giving the alarm in case of a night attack. The place was called Clouds Mills and it was the place where Ellsworth's Zouaves carried on the flour business—perhaps you saw a sketch of it in a pictorial paper. There we had a barricade of barrels filled with sand and piled up in the road, with a mill on our right and a high hill on the left. We took three rebel dragoons—fine-looking fellows—and gave them over to the General in command. They had a flag of truce, which was

considered a mere subterfuge, and they are yet
detained as spies. In the afternoon a boy came
down to the barricade and said a party of rebel
cavalry had carried off his father, who was a
Union man. I rather suspected the boy, but
nevertheless took ten men and proceeded with
great caution about two and a half miles in
the country. Finding by inquiry of negroes
that I was getting within the rebel lines, and
hearing that no such man as was claimed resided there, I turned back, and guess pretty luck-
ily, for that night some rebel cavalry came within a mile of our barricade. I remained at the
mill till Thursday noon, living on the neighbors,
who were all secessionists, but *very accommoda-
ting*. I boarded with a farmer who had two sons
in the Southern army, and who had had a
brother killed in the last battle. His wife, however, put no arsenic in the hoe-cakes, and we
used to smoke pipes together in the grove by
his house. This is a queer state of things, after
all.

I don't know that I ever told you of the fine
present the boys of my company gave me—a
gilt-mounted sword worth twenty-five dollars,
a camp bed that will fold up in a carpet bag,
worth six dollars ; a camp stool, one dollar ; and
two pairs of white military gloves, three dollars.
I got a stray horse the other day off at the mill

and he is around in camp now. A great many
of the soldiers go around here and there on
stray horses which they have picked up.
Where we are now encamped we are within the
range of Fort Ellsworth; so to-morrow we are
to move farther up in the country, in another
range of hills. Where we are now is a beatiful
place. From my window I can see the Potomac
and the Capitol of Washington away off in the
distance—also Alexandria, which now is literally being deserted. I don't believe there'll be
a general engagement again very soon, for I
learn that the Southern army after all is cut up
much worse than ours. Lincoln, Seward and
General McDowell came up to our camp the day
before yesterday, escorted by a troop of cavalry,
and called upon the Colonel. I have seen *him*
now several times—attended two receptions
when in Washington and got introduced to
"Abe" and "Mrs. Abe," the latter of whom is
far the best looking.

I understand that General McClellan is here
now to command the Army of the Potomac. I
have much more confidence in him than in Mc-
Dowell, for we are all of the impression that we
can beat the rebels two to one, on a fair field
and with prudent officers.   GEORGE.

George, from the time of his enlistment, applied himself diligently to the work of mastering military tactics and had become quite proficient in the art. He was also a very popular officer, both with his subordinates and his associates in arms. An officer of his Company in a letter to a friend thus wrote:

"Captain Arrowsmith is the idol of his soldiers. The influence he wields as an officer is remarkable. There is not a man of them but would cheerfully follow him into the very jaws of death. He seldom has occasion to administer a rebuke. An order of his when once understood he is never compelled to repeat, but has the pleasure of seeing it executed with the utmost alacrity."

THE TENTED FIELD.

A N ordinary history of the late war is replete with information concerning the movements and operations of armies, as supplied by corps, division and brigade commanders; but how little is written from the standpoint of the subordinate officer, or the private! George's letters are valuable and instructive in this particular, as a relation not only of the daily occurrences and the *minutiæ* of camp life which engross the attention of the humble soldier, but also as presenting views of the military situation as he sees it.

In the following interesting communications are presented further pen pictures of life on the tented field :

CAMP MAXWELL, VA., August 4th, 1861.

To the Editor of the Utica Morning Herald:

My letters, you will observe, like everything else pertaining to camp, are very irregular. Food in camp is irregular with a moving regiment, both as regards quantity and quality. Sometimes, when shifting our position, we have long fasts, which are not particularly conducive to a prayerful mood ; at other times, potatoes, peaches, chickens, onions, beets, etc., mysteriously appear and disappear around the camp fires. "A moment seen, then gone forever." We do not, as a regiment, generally make a practice of foraging ; but then, if we did not do it a little, Kerrigan's regiment, which is near us, would get more than their "rations." Cattle are very rarely disturbed, though, it is true, horses are occasionally impressed into the service of their country, while a misanthropic mule may sometimes be seen sedately carrying two or three volunteers around on his back. Sleeping is also irregular, and in all sorts of places, from the finest of bedrooms down to the open air, in a rain, with the boots of a neighbor for a pillow. Tents are fine apartments though, except during a heavy rain, when the ground floor is apt to be quite damp, especially if on a low, marshy spot.

Since I wrote last we have been newly uniformed, and have laid aside the old colorless
clothes which the men have so long worn under
protest. Of course this gave an entirely new
appearance to the regiment, which looked as if
it had just been "shedding." One fellow, much
fatigued after a long march, awoke from a long
sleep that afternoon and saw what seemed a lot
of strangers about. *Loquitur*, rubbing his eyes,
" Wh-what regiment's this? Where's the Twenty-sixth? Did you see which way they went?"
We were inspected by a regular officer last Friday, who is going through all the regiments
along the river.

The greatest confidence is felt in all quarters
in the ability and tact of General McClellan; and
his untiring activity imparts a vigor to every
department of the army. The forests are still
being levelled, entrenchments thrown up and
batteries erected. The Northern "mud sills"
are making havoc in the "sacred soil" generally,
enough, at least, to embitter the feelings of even
that part of "the chivalry" who were the best
inclined towards the North. I think the ideas
of the Northern press with reference to Southern sentiment are very erroneous. Around here
the inhabitants seem to be all secessionists, but of
course they are not forward in ventilating their
politics, especially when they are certain that

it will tell upon their hen-roosts and orchards.
A young farmer boy can scarcely be found anywhere around here; all, as I suppose, being off
with the army. The rebel army is made of good
material. The Black Horse Cavalry, especially,
were made up almost wholly of men of culture
and fortune, and I've heard the greatest mortifi-
cation expressed by Virginians that they should
have been cut to pieces by the New York Fire-
men —the aristocracy by the *sans culottes*. These
Zouaves, by the way, are the "lions" among the
troops about here. Their officers are all either
dead or good for nothing, and they warm all
over recounting their adventures and showing
their trophies from the Bull Run battle. The
Zouaves, Kerrigan's, the Mozart, McCunn's, Mc-
Leod Murphy's and Lansing's are the regiments
whose camps are nearest our own.

Mr. Owen J. Lewis of your city was visiting
through our camp yesterday, surrounded, as
you may well imagine, by crowds of old acquaintances asking for news from Utica. A
man in civilian's dress is quite a curiosity now,
and we stare at him with as much interest as
we used to have in a military company, when we
delighted to follow them barefooted through
the streets for miles, to the great disgust of all
school teachers. Mr. Lewis started this morning on a trip to Fortress Monroe.

Colonel Kerrigan was heard to pay Colonel Christian and our regiment quite a compliment the other day. He remarked that it was the best-drilled volunteer regiment he had yet seen.

It is now Sunday night ; warm, oh, how warm, but beautiful! Grim-looking war ships are lying silently in the river between here and Washington. The Chaplain is holding religious services at one end of the camp, with the band putting in " Old Hundred " and " Coronation " occasionally. From another part may be heard soldiers chanting " Dixie," celebrating the virtues of the " Female Smuggler," or bewailing the untimely death of " Gentle Annie." It is half-past nine, and time that these noises stopped—also it's time my light was put out.   ALIQUIS.

There was what was called the " three months trouble " about this time. Men who had enlisted for three months and their time expiring, insisted upon going home and refused to do duty, for which cause there were several arrests. They were assured that as recruiting progressed those anxious to go home might do so, but the necessity for their services was imperative for the time being, and they were required by the Government to report for duty to the Adjutant-General of the United States Army at the expiration of their term of service.

A little later the Colonel of the Twenty-sixth
New York Regiment called about him his officers
and stated that he desired none to remain except such as were prepared to serve the full two
years. Upon this fourteen officers tendered
their resignations, which were at once accepted
and their successors from among those who
were "in for the war" selected.

The next letter is from Camp Maxwell,
Virginia, under date of August 7th, 1861:

To the Editor of the Utica Morning Herald:

We were aroused again last night by two
couriers from General McClellan, who ordered
us to assemble, with the rest of the brigade, immediately along the Leesburg road. This was
a little after midnight, and we lay out until
morning, but got into no engagement. We
could hear the rumbling of their artillery
wagons, however, and it is known that some part
of the rebel army is not far distant. These infantry regiments in an alarm in the night turn
out very quietly, and, as they have no lights, a
person might be not more than fifty yards from
the camp and not know that a man was astir.
If we are attacked here a battery will be sent
across to Washington, in apprehension, I suppose, of feigned attacks. This lying out in case

of alarm is what the boys call "going out to pasture," and it isn't very pleasing when they are obliged to sleep in the wet grass all night, and then return to camp in the morning without any engagement.

The following order was read on parade, last evening, by the Colonel :

His Excellency, the President of the United States, desiring the further service of the Twenty-Sixth Regiment, New York State Volunteers, and having made requisition upon the Governor of this State, therefore, Colonel Christian is hereby directed, on the expiration of the term for which such regiment was mustered into the service of the United States, (August 21st, 1861), to report with his command to the Adjutant-General of the United States Army, for duty under the order of the United States Government for the remainder of the term of enlistment of the regiment into the service of the State of New York.

By order of the Commander-in-Chief,

D. CAMPBELL,
Assistant Adjutant-General.

This occasions a great deal of disappointment among the men, many of whom had made arrangements to go to their homes after the twenty-first of August. The Colonel, however, says that as recruiting progresses those very anxious to go home may gradually all get a discharge, as he will use his exertions for that object at the War Department. He believes that the war at most will not last a year, and is determined himself at all events to see its close in the service.

The following changes have occurred in the officer roll of the Twenty-Sixth Regiment, and we much regret that those resigned now are leaving us. The appointments, which have been made from among the most trustworthy and reliable men in the regiment, have been confirmed by Governor Morgan, and the new officers will enter upon the discharge of their duties immediately. The resignations were assented to by General McDowell, and the officers resigning discharged from the service of the United States :

William K. Bacon, Adjutant, vice David Smith, Jr., resigned.

Ensign Gilbert A. Hay, Lieutenant of Company A, vice William A. Mercer, resigned.

Sergeant-Major John T. Kingsbury, Ensign of Company A, vice Hay, promoted.

Lieutenant Norman W. Palmer, Captain of Company E, vice Antoine Brendle, resigned.

Ensign H. D. Barnett, Lieutenant of Company B, vice Norman W. Palmer, promoted.

Sergeant William J. Harlow, Ensign of Company B, vice Barnett, promoted.

Sergeant William C. Gardner, Lieutenant of Company D, vice William P. West, promoted.

Lieutenant E. R. P. Shurly, of Company G,

Captain of Company C, vice John H. Fairbanks, resigned.

Sergeant Hugh Leonard, Ensign of Company D, vice Richard Hall, resigned.

Sergeant Charles B. Coventry, Lieutenant of Company E, vice Oliver W. Sheldon, resigned.

Corporal Charles Smith, Ensign of Company E, vice James VanVleck, resigned.

Corporal William Cone, Lieutenant of Company F, vice Rufus D. Patten, resigned.

Private John Williams, Ensign of Company F, vice John Bevine, resigned.

Ensign Frank L. Binder, Lieutenant of Company G, vice E. R. P. Shurly, promoted.

Frank Lee, Ensign of Company G, vice Binder, promoted.

Lieutenant William P. West, Captain of Company I, vice John H. Palmer, resigned.

Corporal Alonzo Thompson, Lieutenant of Company I, vice Henry J. Flint, resigned.

Charles S. Johnson, Ensign of Company I, vice John W. Kinney, resigned.

Ensign Emmet Harder, Lieutenant of Company K, vice Charles F. Baragar, resigned.

Sergeant Albert D. Lynch, Ensign of Company K, vice Harder, promoted.

ALIQUIS.

(The officers as above appointed have been duly commissioned by Governor Morgan.)

August 18th, 1861, we find the Twenty-sixth at Alexandria again, and Aliquis writes as fol·lows :

ALEXANDRIA, August 18th, 1861.

To the Editor of the Utica Morning Herald :

We have again moved our camp, in order to join the brigade to which we have been annexed —General Heintzelman's. We have thus lost the beautiful grounds and the splendid scenery of our former location ; but we are glad to find ourselves in a brigade where affairs will be con·ducted with more system. This moving a regi·ment after it gets well settled down, is a great nuisance, and makes much confusion for a short time. If we only had some women to scold the teamsters, it would be as good as an ordinary May Day. The army drivers use only one line to their four horses, and this occasions the use of quite a variety of terms to their horses, which increases to a most hideous jargon whenever about a dozen teamsters get tangled up in a stumpy field. All the camp articles are thrown into these large wagons in beautiful confusion. Through the opening in the rear of the wagons may be seen a musket, a man's leg, a knapsack and a camp pail. Two men march with each wagon to guard it, and away they go, the regi·ment just ahead of them. Well, when we get

to the new ground, the wagons are unloaded in
the rain, (for it is always as sure to rain when
we "move" as it is when a Sabbath-school gets
up a picnic)—then the companies go to work
putting up their tents, and after the usual
amount of shouting and quarrelling, things
finally settle down into the old order. Enterprising men then make a variety of fire-places
in the ground, into which some *very* luxurious
individual may place a joint of stove pipe. Perhaps the same pampered person that revels amid
these conveniences may get some boards off
from a fence and put a floor in his tent to sleep
upon ; but most of us live like plain volunteers.
I suppose it is very novel and pleasant around
in York state for your military companies to
"camp out" about a week in nice weather, with
buffalo robes and champagne, and stand guard,
watching in great suspicion for the approach
of an enemy from a neighboring corn field.
But "camping out" loses its novelty after a
few months, and standing guard becomes a
stern reality when it is known that Jackson's
brothers can't be broken of their very impolite
habit of shooting our pickets. Every one of
these volunteers whom the Northern citizens
encouraged to go to war for their country, and
whom you cheered and told to shoot Jeff Davis,
and whom you gave five dollars and advised

not to get killed, ole feller—though they never
get into a pitched battle, are nevertheless entitled to great credit for the instances of self-
denial in their lives as soldiers. The volunteers
are now the only force the country can rely
upon. The regular army is now only a fossil
relic of something that *once* was of some importance. Now it is only of use as a police
force, for which it is usually employed. Colonel
Christian had occasion the other day to express nearly these same opinions to a regular
captain, and he "owned the corn," expressing
his preference for the volunteers. Strange to
say, political favoritism is exhibited as much
as ever in the army appointments. Young sons
of rich politicians, who bid fair to be good
for nothing else, can usually be lieutenants in
the army. In the style of fighting which this
war brings out, men will have to act as individuals very often with the lines broken, and
the personal identity of the men ought not to
be swallowed up in the regiment, as is too much
the result of the intellect-deadening drill in the
regular army. Hurrah for the volunteer!

Our brigade is composed of four regiments,
the Sixteenth, Twenty-sixth and Twenty-seventh
New York, and the Fifth Maine. General
Heintzleman is quite unwell, and is at Washington, while Colonel Davis is at present in com-

mand. Colonel Christian is the second in rank.
Our situation is to the extreme south of the
Army of the Potomac, and our pickets extend
nearly down to Mount Vernon. The regiments
in the brigade take turns sending out pickets,
and the companies in the regiment take turns
going. Three of our companies have gone out
to-day with two field pieces. Before we left our
old camp our pickets out by Bailey's Cross
Roads had a sort of skirmish with some rebel
horsemen. We lost no men, but as near as we
could learn from the inhabitants around there,
and what our men themselves saw, six of the
enemy were unhorsed. I met an old schoolmate at the Provost Marshal's, the other day,
under arrest as a spy. He was very glad to see
me, and in talking over old times we forgot
that it was our duy to cut each other's throats.
His name is John Bradley; he lives in Alexandria, and is a secessionist. " Sich is life."

ALIQUIS.

DESTRUCTION OF A BRIDGE.

CAPTAIN ARROWSMITH and his company acting under orders take an active part in the destruction of the bridge over Hunting Run to prevent its use by the enemy and the capture of Alexandria. A description of this affair is contained in a communication to the *Utica Herald* from Alexandria under date of August 18th, 1861, but not from the pen of Aliquis, as follows :

HEADQUARTERS 26TH N. Y. VOLUNTEERS, }
ALEXANDRIA, VA., August 18th. }

To the Editor of the Utica Morning Herald:

A brief description of two nights' duty and the destruction of the bridge over Hunting Run will no doubt be interesting to you.

OUR SITUATION.

A mile or two below Alexandria a great bay

sets back from the Potomac into the western
shore ; on the north it bends around a promon-
tory until it edges upon the suburbs of the city,
while upon the south are high and wooded lands,
threaded by a score of roads leading to the
enemy's camp only a few miles distant. The
Mount Vernon road which crosses this important
bridge intersects all these roads.

The bridge was nearly half a mile in length,
consisting of a causeway from either shore several rods in length, connected by a substantial
oaken structure, and crossed the Run about one
mile from the Potomac.

A sluggish stream winds through the meadows
at the base of the hills, emptying into the Run
about two miles from the river. This stream
and the Run are known as "Hunting Run."
They form the dividing line of the two great
armies on the south of our position.

The camps of the Sixteenth, Twenty-sixth and
Twenty-seventh New York Volunteers and Fifth
Maine, are located in the meadow, just upon the
northern edge of these waters.

ONE NIGHT'S DUTY.

Last Sunday the Colonel sent three companies
across the bridge, conducted by Captains Jennings, West and Blackwell ; these companies
separated on the opposite side, each taking

different roads, and proceeding from four to six
miles toward the enemy, threw out their pickets
and remained till next morning

About two o'clock in the morning they faintly
heard voices apparently giving commands in
the distance. Captain Jennings cautiously approached a mile beyond, and plainly heard the
deadened tramp of a large column of infantry.

It was late in the day of Monday when the
companies came back to camp. The Colonel,
upon hearing their report, immediately mounted
his horse and, accompanied by Lieutenant-
Colonel Richardson and Major Jennings, went
to the bridge, and to their surprise found it
guarded by only nine men of the Twenty-seventh
New York Regiment. Proceeding to the headquarters of General Franklin, Colonel Christian
reported the case, and asked permission to become responsible for the security of the road
against any approach of the enemy: for this
duty it was determined to send a company.

A NIGHT IN THE RAIN.

Captain Arrowsmith, upon his request, was
assigned this duty. Adjutant Bacon also accompanied them as a volunteer. The night was
one of the most dismal I ever saw; the rain fell
in torrents. The men were obliged to stand
along the bridge, exposed to the full vigor of

the storm—while the fearless Captain and our
promising young Adjutant occasionally crossed
toward the hills and listened for an expected
approach. Red and yellow rockets were re-
peatedly thrown from the camps of the enemy,
which marked a chain of regiments from the
river for several miles towards Manassas. In
the morning the company returned to camp,
and, notwithstanding their sleepless night, as
usual went through the duties of the day.

THE DESTRUCTION OF THE BRIDGE.

In the edge of last evening, by invitation of
Colonel Christian, I accompanied him for the
first time to the bridge. We then called on
Colonel Davies (at present commanding this
Brigade), to whom the Colonel plainly stated
the negligence in allowing the bridge to remain
—how easily with a howitzer the enemy could
sweep our infantry from it—and remarked that
we were carrying on the war as though we
would not inconvenience the enemy, injure his
property, or hurt any of them, and proposed
that we take the responsibility of destroying the
bridge. The Colonel's assent being given, two
companies, one of the Twenty-sixth and the
other of the Twenty-seventh, proceeded to the
work, and this morning saw but a few forlorn
timbers where yesterday stood a noble structure.

Thus war compels the destruction in a day of many works which have cost months of labor; but in destroying this bridge we cut off one of the most feasible approaches of the enemy upon Alexandria.

Adjutant William Kirkland Bacon referred to in the above letter was a warm friend of Captain Arrowsmith. He was only nineteen years of age, and had left Hamilton College to enroll himself as a private in defence of his country. He is described as the soul of honor and possessed of an unsullied personal purity. He distinguished himself by his bravery upon a number of battle-fields, receiving a grievous wound at Manassas, and falling mortally wounded at the battle of Fredericksburgh.

In a private letter to his parents, Adjutant Bacon writes concerning the guarding of the bridge over Hunting Run where he served with Captain Arrowsmith as follows :

" Four or five days ago I accompanied Captain Arrowsmith, with part of his men and a number from Company C, in charge of Ensign Neill, to guard a bridge which crosses Hunting Run and connects Alexandria with the Mount Vernon road. The night was dark and stormy, and the rain fell in torrents. Before morning I was

drenched to the skin, and my comrades fared no
better. My revolver and sword became wet,
and the next day were so rusty that it took
several hours to clean them. I do not think the
Captain and myself, who are quite intimate
friends, thought very much at the time of the
importance of the mission on which we were
sent. We sat together, and talked about all the
old times at home, and contrasted our condition
at the time with the pleasant, cheerful firesides
there, where we could easily enjoy the greatest
comfort and luxury in the world. How foolish,
we thought, would we be considered if we should
even run out for a few moments in the rain at
home. Here, however, we were doing what was
rendering our country some little service. If
the secessionists had obtained possession of the
bridge, they could have taken Alexandria without a blow, and, it might be, have caused another
such disastrous rout as that at Bull's Run. We
had really the distinguished honor of volunteer-
ing to protect (with our lives if need be) one of
the most important outposts of the Federal
army. When one sees how much the country
needs his services at this crisis, can he, with
any degree of self-satisfaction, consent to return
home, however much he would love to see once
more those whom he has left behind ? For my
own part, sooner than leave the service of my

country, to which I am indebted for the bless-
ings of freedom and almost unbounded liberty,
I would consent to die the worst of deaths. Our
country is now passing through a most terribly
trying ordeal, but I hope she will come out puri-
fied by the test. God is on our side, and with
His help we will forever crush out the hydra-
headed monster of secession; and, I hope, settle,
once and for all, the question—so often agitated
—of slavery.

"We will probably remain here for about a
month longer, and then advance towards Manassas. The great army, thousands of which are
now pouring into Washington daily, will soon
be ready to take the places of the regiments
now stationed here and all along this side of the
Potomac. It may be that the rebels, anticipat-
ing our advance, will make a counter movement,
and attempt to force our lines back upon Washington, or further if possible. This, however, I
do not think will be done, for, if accounts are
true, the rebel army is in a far worse state
of demoralization than ours. The payment of
troops in scrip and corporation currency—such
as we used to call 'shinplasters'—must be suf-
ficient of itself to cause complaint and dissatisfaction. It is said, too, that as the Confederate
election must soon take place, Davis, Lee and
Beauregard are at 'sword's points.' This would

not be very unnatural, for three men as ambitious as they are never pull well together."

The following extract is from a letter of
George to his father, dated September 1st, 1861,
from Alexandria, Camp Vernon, expressing his
desire not to miss any work :

"This brigade is the extreme left of the army
here.   I'm picketing and scouting and have been
down on the Washington estates and in view of
Mount Vernon.

"It seems to me that summer has passed very
quickly; to-day is the first of autumn.   What
fighting there is to be done will have to be done
up before January I suppose.   If we go into
winter quarters then I'll come home on furlough
right away, but at present I'm afraid that I'd
just miss all the work if I should leave now.
We are daily expecting an engagement and we
are confident as to the result.   We see balloons,
rockets and fires in the rebel camp nearly every
night.   I went the other night so near them
with some pickets that we beat up a 'long roll'
in their camp which we could hear distinctly.

"I'm now 'color captain,' that is, occupy the
position in line just to the right of the centre.
I am well and hard at work."

A DESCRIPTION OF ALEXANDRIA.

THE following bright letter contains among other things a flash-light picture of Alexandria :

ALEXANDRIA, VA., September 3d, 1861.

To the Editor of the Utica Morning Herald :

Alexandria is an old-looking town to a Northerner. An old-looking place it is, and in this the Virginians take great pride, and they speak of the reputation it had as a shipping port in the Revolution. There is the old engine house of the Friendship Company, to which one George Washington, of Mount Vernon, once belonged. Here is the road along which Braddock proceeded on his ill-fated expedition. But one needs some such recollections to divert his attention, for it abounds in unpleasant odors of

all descriptions. Every corner we turn there
appears to be a new smell, and even the drug
stores present their unfavorable side to the pas-
senger. There is only one thing worse in Alexandria than its odor, and that is its pavements.
If a new geographer should come on its streets,
and not know it was intentionally paved, he
would term it a "very rough and rocky region,
and only visited by travelers with great risks."
But Alexandria was really paved, a part of it
during the Revolutionary War, and there have
been no essential repairs since. It is, however,
called by the natives "a right smart chance of a
town." It abounds in negroes, drug stores,
confectioneries, mosquitoes, and at present, soldiers. The military police seem as omnipresent,
I suppose, as those of Paris—ferreting out spies,
searching buildings for concealed arms, arrest-
ing disorderly soldiers, and confining gentlemen
who venture around too much without a pass,
sending them to the Provost Marshal's, very
red and indignant, between two muskets. The
"slave pen," once the scene of the liveliest trade
in Alexandria, is now used as a military prison.
Courts Martial are now a fixed institution in the
town, and it is very interesting to attend them
and witness the examination of suspected citizens, spies, and deserters. The Seventeenth
New York Regiment is now occupying and

guarding the town; Fort Ellsworth, which they formerly held, being now manned by a strong body of sailors.

Out by Bailey's Cross Roads, both armies are at work night and day, throwing up intrench-ments right in sight of each other. Over a thousand men on each side are continually wielding the pickaxe and spade, preparing, I suppose, for a battle near Washington, which is inevitably to decide the contest. There is occa-sionally a shot exchanged just by way of recog-nition to officers who visit the works on horse-back. Colonel Christian, accompanied by other officers, frequently rides out to view the progress of the intrenchments.

Big time among the boys yesterday. Found three "feminine" ambrotypes in the bottom of a box of clothing that had never before been overhauled ; startling effect upon the personal appearance of the troops from these ambrotypes : thanks to the fair unknown who have furnished these "three episodes," as Ward would call them.

Our regiment now have the black army hats of the style of the seventeenth century, with plumes and ornaments. If the men were only waist deep in the water, they would pass very well for the "Landing of the Pilgrims." The volunteer force is gradually becoming uniform

in its dress, a thing which the Bull Run experience shows to be most desirable.

I have been much disappointed with the climate of Virginia. For the last three weeks there
has been but little warm weather, and the nights
are indeed quite cold. Those who came South
illy provided with clothing have made a great
mistake, and it is probably these deluded persons that we hear practising "double quick" up
and down the company streets towards morning.

The two years' excitement has all subsided,
and the daily expectation of a battle absorbs
everything else. "Give us something to do,"
the men say, "and we will stay cheerfully as
long as necessary." There is every probability
that the old regiments *will* have something to
do in the autumn campaign, for it will doubtless
be the policy of the General to leave the lately
formed regiments to protect Washington. You
may rest assured that this regiment is none the
less eager for service, and no less patriotic on
account of the crisis through which this, in common with many others, has passed. Leave a
wide margin for exaggeration in estimating the
reliability of news from Washington, for it is
verily a city of sensations. We are really
obliged to look in the New York papers to get
the news from the army, and in fact, they get up
incidents so much better, and tell of feats so

much more gallant and escapes so much more
miraculous than we hear of here, that it is very
pleasant to get information through that channel.
I heard it rumored last night that General Mc-
Dowell was arrested for treason.

ALIQUIS.

A reason for the inactivity complained of in
the last letter was the fact that the Twenty-sixth
Regiment was too well disciplined to be spared
from the force reserved for the protection of
Washington, though the Colonel and other
officers had made strenuous efforts to be allowed
to join the advancing army. They were not
idle, however. They built and occupied Fort
Lyon, then one of the strongest fortifications of
the kind in Virginia.

BEAUTIFUL CAMP MARY.

THE regiment's camp is now moved to a more comfortable place, near the bank of the Potomac, where Aliquis discusses various regimental matters.

CAMP MARY, September 12th, 1861.

To the Editor of the Utica Morning Herald:

Again we have moved, and this time to a beautiful piece of ground to which Colonel Christian has given the name that heads this letter. It is over Hunting Run, where we have moved, which carries us still more to the left of the Grand Army of the Potomac—the left regiment in the left Brigade. We are now under the command of General Slocum, an officer of whom we all have the highest ideas. Letters to the regiment, however, still occasionally come directed to Colonel McCunn or General Heintzleman's Brigade, an error which correspondents should take care to correct. Our Brigade is to be posted behind a line of intrenchments, and nearly our whole force is working on them every day; we already have a fine rifle pit in our front. Our regiment came up yesterday afternoon, and last night was the only one on this side of the river. In the evening some picket firing off in front of us kept us on the alert for a while ; nothing serious, however, occurred, though it is reported to-day that some of the Maine boys were captured. To-day the rest of the Brigade have been moving up, together with a company of dragoons, and Captain Thompson's battery, so that affairs now look a little more sociable. We now really are finely situated, and we have taken great care to make the camp comfortable. An unoccupied house near by was taken down to make floors to the tents, the fences in the neighborhood being rather defective. Captain Palmer has charge of a squad of men daily employed in making a log building for the convenience of the guard, facetiously called " Fort Palmer." Yesterday afternoon we heard the skirmish up at the other end of the line, of which you have of course heard, but reported fighting is now so common a topic that it creates but little interest.

Picketing is a favorite duty with the men and officers of the regiment. There is a most solemn stillness along the roads that lead from Alexandria down into the country, and you may travel miles and see scarcely a living being, and hear only the chirping of insects or the singing of birds. I lay out all night not long since, on a hill at the outposts of the Federal lines. I never saw a more beautiful landscape. As the moon rose up slowly and made the still Potomac appear as a flare of light, the stillness had a drowsy effect upon us all. I lay, thinking of the prospect of a fight, when five horsemen, armed to the teeth, suddenly rode up to my comrade and myself, and ordered us to surrender. Knowing the danger of grasping my musket, I did not make the attempt, but rising suddenly, I seized the leader by the throat—"Look here, you thunderin' fool, if you don't sleep a little more quiet, you'll get punched in the eye!" I'll never forgive Jim for spoiling that heroic dream.

Mortimer Thompson, "Doesticks," has been rusticating in our regiment for two or three weeks, and is an "honorary member" of the Colonel's staff. He is continually scouring over the country, going out with the pickets, etc., and seems to be in love with soldiering.

The three months' question has now "gone glimmering in the dream of things that were," and the regiment is running like clockwork. I am obliged to inform you that no men were shot for insubordination, at the risk, however, of spoiling the effect of some fine newspaper paragraphs. Our Adjutant proves himself a very active and able officer, and has become very popular in the regiment. The Colonel and the company officers are continually in receipt of letters from mothers, wives and fathers of soldiers soliciting discharges and furloughs for them. They seem to have a sort of vague idea that the officers can just summarily send the men home in a " Depart, go in peace " style. At most, all the Colonel can do is to make application for the discharges, which he knows very well would never be granted, unless in cases of marked physical debility. To give every letter received due attention, would require the individual efforts of every officer in the regiment, for a discharge has to be "lobbied" through like a bill in the Legislature. Besides these applications, there are innumerable applications for officers' positions. Young John Smith or some one has just got his education ; his father Mr. Smith or some one, a man of high respectability, wishes him to fight for the honor of his country's flag, but at the same time does not wholly undervalue the "loaves and fishes." Young John is described as not being altogether

inexperienced in military, having been fourth
corporal in the Tenth Wide Awakes, and has
witnessed several encampments of the Smithville
Blues, therefore an application is made that
Smith may have an office, that eventually he
may become General McSmith perhaps. Our
regiment has in its non-commissioned officers
and privates ample material for good officers,
and it is really unjust to them that strangers'
claims should be preferred to the claims of those
whose previous stations and course of duty
render them eligible to the positions. This is
the principle which the Colonel evidently aims
to observe in the selection of his officers.

Our regiment now numbers eight hundred and
thirty men, and some recruits we learn are now
on their way here. We have had comparatively
little sickness amongst us, and no deaths by disease that I am aware of. Our band from Roch-
ester has been discharged, and that seems to
leave a vacant place in the regiment. But really
a brass band, like an elephant, is a cumbersome
sort of luxury to keep. They are not expected
to fight, and yet a base drum for instance is not
a handy thing to move with when cavalry are in
pursuit. We have occasionally to suffer some
loss from disability and a committee sits every
Monday in Alexandria to receive applications for
discharges.   ALIQUIS.

A VISIT TO MOUNT VERNON.

THE next contribution from the pen of Aliquis contains a charming description of his visit to Mount Vernon.

CAMP MARY, September 19th, 1861.
To the Editor of the Utica Morning Herald:

Since my last letter, I have visited Mount Vernon, and have "done" all the sights and wonders of that place. This place is not now occupied by rebels, but is occasionally visited by scouting parties of both sides. We enter the Mount Vernon farm long before we get to the mansion itself, which is surrounded by quite large forests. The farm, as originally held by the General, consisted of 7,600 acres now owned by a large number of persons, mostly of Northern birth — from New York and New Jersey.

The residence of Washington was indeed most
beautiful.   Nature here is profuse in her gifts,
and the finest taste was exhibited in the plan
and the decorations of the place—everything
ample and spacious, and no doubt these magnificent surroundings have had their influence
in preserving in Washington that noble love of
nature and humanity for which he was so noted.

Well, my friend and I come up to the mansion
and are escorted by a lady of the Association,
who informs us that we are requested to leave
our muskets at the house while we go about the
grounds.   We take a suspicious look about us,
and with a ghastly smile consent to let the lady
keep our guns ; not, however, without some
reluctance.   We then, after taking another
cautious look around us, proceed to weep duly
over the tomb of Washington, taking the precaution, however, to assure ourselves that it is
not the ice house, which much resembles it, and
which we understand is sometimes "lingered
over" with much sadness by foreign tourists.
The tomb is really in a sad condition, and rank
weeds are intruding themselves through the iron
grate that forms the door.   There are near the
tomb monuments of other members of the family,
among them that of Judge Bushrod Washington.
The out-houses around the grounds are about
twenty-five in number, and not one but that had

the appearance of being constructed with a view
to ornament as well as utility. After parading
around the grounds very grandly, and imagining
ourselves General Washington taking a walk
before breakfast, we proceed to view the main
house, which is much larger than I supposed.
The first thing that strikes us is the key of the
Bastile, hanging in a case on the wall. After
informing another visitor that the Bastile was
not a smoke house and that this was not the key
of the smoke house, we pass through the ample
rooms and see the old pictures, the holsters, the
saddles, the surveyor's tripod, and finally the
harpsichord made in Cheapside, London, which
we essay to play upon, to the great amusement
of "Mount Vernon's Association." We then express a wish to go up stairs, but are forbidden
by the attendant, who informs us that the upper
story is occupied by the ladies, so we are denied
the pleasure of seeing the antique specimens
there congregated.

I returned from Mount Vernon, hardly able
to realize that I had been there—hardly able to
realize that one was obliged to visit the tomb of
our country's founder and Father, armed against
a treason participated in by descendants of his
own family —hardly able to realize that Washington's remains lie in the neutral ground between two mighty armies, each claiming to as-

semble in defense of the principles for which he
labored.

The enemy now seem to be most near us in
the direction of Fairfax. The Colonel, the Adjutant and Captain Palmer, with four dragoons,
rode out yesterday until they saw an encampment of them and some artillery, over beyond
Bush Hill. While the party were there, General
McClellan, at Fort Taylor, ordered some shells
to be thrown at the enemy, which exploded not
far from them. The enemy, the Colonel says,
responded in defiance with a field piece.

General McClellan comes around visiting the
camps occasionally, and seems to be particularly
interested in strengthening the left flank of the
army. He was in our camp last Tuesday, and
he, in company with Colonels Christian and
Bartlett, visited the pickets and outposts of our
brigade. Those acquainted with him report
him to be a sociable, modest man, much addicted
to joking and smoking, but of fine sensibilities.

We are daily expecting to have our muskets
exchanged for the Springfield rifles. Probably
in a general engagement, a musket would be
preferable to a rifle, as they become clogged less
easily, and may be fired with greater rapidity ;
but for scouting or skirmishing, rifles are far
superior. Since I last wrote, one of our men has
been very badly wounded, having been shot

while wandering beyond our pickets on the Richmond road. Two men rose from behind a log, and coolly firing at him ran away themselves, not daring to approach him after he was lying on the ground. This barbarous custom of shooting outposts does not seem to abate much, and they hunt each other like Indians. At one point the rebel pickets are on one side of a peach orchard and ours on the other ; so that between the two, the fruit does not get much stolen. At another point, the federal troops occupy a church in the day time, and the rebels at night ; and they both keep their hours with remarkable precision.

The fort upon which we are at work every day will be by far the largest on this side of the river, and will cover several acres of ground. It is on a fine hill, commanding a view of Fort Ellsworth, Fort Taylor, and a rebel post on Mason's Hill. About two thousand men are at work with the picks and spades every day.

ALIQUIS.

SKIRMISH AT POHICH CHURCH.

I AM indebted to Mr. Stephen V. Arrowsmith
for the following account of a skirmish, in
which two companies commanded by Captain
Arrowsmith were engaged at a place called
Pohich Church, where after a rough march of
eight miles before daylight he surprises the
enemy at daybreak and captures what was most
desirable at that immediate juncture—an invit-
ing breakfast.

"At the skirmish of Pohich Church, he was
the officer in command, and conducted two
companies of his regiment over a new country for a distance of seven or eight miles to surprise, and if possible, capture a company of
rebel cavalry who were quartered in the church
and who were robbing and plundering the Union

farmers in the vicinity. On approaching the
church, they found one of the rebel pickets,
who was posted at some distance from the
church, in order to guard against surprise. As
soon as he could see by the imperfect light (for
it was just at daybreak in the morning), that
the approaching body were Unionists, he immediately rode in and gave the alarm to his
companions, who were just in the act of sitting
down to enjoy their warm breakfast of the best
and most substantial fare that the neighboring rich farms could produce. The surprise
was complete. The alarm was given—the bugle
sounded 'To Horse!' and they immediately
mounted their horses and stood in readiness to
resist an attack.

"George drew his men up in line and gave
the command 'Fire!' when several of the rebels
were seen to roll from their horses, and the rest
retreated across a field and dismounted behind
a fence, where they fired several ineffectual
volleys and fled. George, in the meantime,
marched his men into the church, where they
took possession of the still untouched and invit-
ing breakfast and refreshed themselves after
their long and tiresome march."

A WAR CAMP IN AUTUMN.

THE season is now well advanced. The nights are getting cold, and fires are blazing in the evening, amid the festivities of camp life. The bracing air revives the spirits of the soldiers and they are eager for a great army movement. The following letters are descriptive of an autumn war camp :

CAMP FRANKLIN, VA., October 15th, 1861.
To the Editor of the Utica Morning Herald :

The organization of divisions has again compelled us to move, so that I now almost regard myself a second Wandering Jew. We now seem to be situated right in the center of the army, near the Fairfax Seminary—have but little picketing to do, and no picking on intrenchments, and the latter, I assure you, is regarded as no privation. Another brigade is now at work finishing Fort Lyon, and ours has again resumed drilling.

The nights are now getting very cold, and every stitch of clothing available is put into use. You may realize what I mean by taking a single blanket and sleeping out on the piazza some night—any one who wishes to try it. Yet a great many soldiers in the army now are unable to get that single blanket even, though the department at Washington is evidently making great efforts to supply them. Overcoats are also very scarce in some of the regiments ; but I understand there is soon to be an abundant supply of them. Comfortable camp fires are now made in the evening, and the bracing air seems to put the men around them in the best of spirits. In one direction I hear there is a lively quadrille, and a fiddler, with a vivid imagination, calling out, "Ladies change!" and "Ladies to the right!" with the utmost gravity. A great many in the regiment have fixed fire places in their tents, in the following manner : A trench is dug, four or five feet long, one end within and the other outside the tent. This is covered with stones or bricks, and a piece of pipe or a barrel connects with the opening outside, to carry off the smoke. At the inner opening a fire is made, which heats up a tent very well, and very rarely

turns any smoke on the inside—unless, of course,
an old hat or a board is found to be placed over
the pipe *outside*. This is fine weather now for a
great movement of some kind, and we suppose
one is soon to be made. Last Saturday every
one expected a battle; the rebels had made a
sudden advance, but they made as sudden a
withdrawal immediately afterward.

Most of the officers of this regiment on last
fast day made a resolution to abstain from the
use of all intoxicating liquors, which is at least
one "forward movement" made. While at work
on the fort, a gill of whiskey was dealt out to
each man every day, which sometimes proved
ruinous to all discipline and order. However,
that is now all stopped. As a general thing
there is but very little drunkenness to be seen
through the army, considering the circumstances.

In obedience to orders recently issued, many
horses and other valuable property which had
been taken from the "Secesh" by our officers
and men have been given up to headquarters,
and some have thereby returned to their owners.
Much of this sort of property, however, has been
sold to the government in Washington, or ship-
ped north. It seems to me to be the very worst
feature of war—the deleterious influence it must
have on the morals of a people, for the- distinc

tion between military pillaging and stealing is
often very fine and subtle.   Those families just
between the two armies have really a dangerous
and harassed life. They endeavor, of course, to
take a neutral course, which only subjects them
to occasional marauds from both parties, and
sometimes skirmishes around their dwellings.
Many wealthy families have been driven to very
coarse living, owing to the stoppage of communication with the towns, and begin to realize
the folly of Virginia in making her soil the battle ground.   There is many an aristocratic family
here who are secessionists, I believe, just for the
sake of keeping their reputation as F. F. V.'s.
Many of these, by the way, own dilapidated,
worn out old farms, and manage to keep up
a sort of Turveydrop gentility only by selling
negroes. However scarce the cash or shabby
the servants, there must be a fine dwelling-house
with a spacious door-yard and very showy entrance. Here these hospitable Virginians sit and
muse on the antiquity and respectability of their
families, and show their visitors their household
relics. I have seen at least a dozen pianos, each
of which was the first ever brought into Virginia,
and numerous clocks which had once belonged
to George Washington. I think the old General
must have had a way of giving furniture to all
of his acquaintances, instead of locks of hair,

when he was getting old, by the *souvenirs* I find. The Virginia gentleman is very hospitable, and if you'll only praise his horses, and not tamper with his negroes, he'll treat you finely, without asking your politics. At present his situation makes him very politic, and he treats officers of both armies out of the same bottle, and often the same day. So much for our "Secesh" acquaintances in Virginia. A broken-winded bugler is now making night hideous, by way of informing us that it is time the lights were out —so here goes!   ALIQUIS.

Four days later he writes to his brother from the same place : "It is now nearly midnight and it is raining very hard, but I have now got fixed so that the weather does not bother me. I have a 'contraband' whom I got out beyond the pickets—a very faithful fellow, who has made a rude floor to my tent, and a kind of bed for me under which he sleeps contentedly. Besides the 'contraband' and the bed, the furniture of my tent consists of a trunk, a large box for company clothing, a stand, a fine armed chair which I got from the officer's quarters out at Pohich church in a foray which we made against the rebels—a box of tobacco, and sundry small articles. We have moved again since I last wrote and are no longer on the left flank, but

near the centre of the army—a situation requir-
ing not so much vigilance as the other. We are
in Slocum's brigade and General Franklin's division, which you may as well notice in directing
your letters. Kearney's New Jersey brigade is
not far from us and they have an excellent reputation. I saw Captain Mount, of Freehold, the
other day in Alexandria where his company is
performing guard duty. Our brigade has now
of course got through working on Fort Lyon
and has gone to drilling again. This afternoon I
watched a balloon reconnoissance by some æro-
naut, who came down just before dark near our
camp."

CAMP FRANKLIN, VA., Nov. 10th, 1861.

To the Editor of the Utica Morning Herald:

Camp life is now dull, most excruciatingly
dull. Where we are now situated we feel about
as secure as we did at Elmira, and have almost
forgotten what we came here for—the chief object of the campaign being, in appearance, to
keep warm. All who have any good pretext are
endeavoring to get leaves of absence, and some
successfully. As for me, my wife and children
are so provokingly healthy, and my appetite so
wofully good, that I am obliged to remain here,
disgusted with the general inactivity, and wondering what will turn up next.

I notice that the ladies of the North are already responding to the numerous calls for
blankets with a renewed liberality. The little
town of Taberg, for instance, with not over five
hundred voters, has sent Company E two immense boxes of useful clothing, consisting chiefly
of blankets and socks. The former were particularly acceptable, but not more so than a large
number of bottles containing "hospital stores,"
known in times of peace as elderberry wine and
brandy. The above large donation was, I learn,
made by the ladies of Taberg and vicinity,
under the auspices of a Mrs. Ingersoll of the
above place. I was enthusiastically informed
of this by Lieutenant Coventry, Charles Beach
and Frank Ingersoll of Company E, whose
happy faces were only equalled by my own,
when I, being in the hospital, had inspected the
aforesaid "stores." But there was also "a epi-
sode," as Ward says, at my tent, followed by
several more "episodes." I refer to blankets,
bedticks, etc., which some unknown lady friends
have sent me. I havn't heard a reveille since.
The box from Mrs. Rockwell and her friends, I
understand, is now in the express office. The
patriotism of these ladies is only equalled by
that of those who, remembering us that are sick,
sent on the "hospital stores."

Colonel Christian arrived in camp yesterday,

having just returned from a two days' leave of
absence ·in New York city. It is strongly
suspected that he has been perpetrating mar-
riage, but no court-martial has yet been con-
vened on the subject. It is earnestly hoped that
no such deleterious example should be held up
before our volunteers, nevertheless rumor says
that he has really taken the "oath of allegiance
to the Union," and been duly "sworn into the
service."

Seven companies of our regiment have to-day
just returned from the outposts, where they have
been picketing for the last four days, some of
them at Annandale. Some of the Twenty-third
regiment were cut off while they were out, but
ours were not seriously disturbed.

Since I last wrote, we have changed the situation of our camp merely to get out of the mud,
into which we were fast sinking in our old place.
The weather is still rather cool and rainy, and
sometimes very heavy frosts are found in the
morning. Many of the men now have little
stoves in the tents, which are much better than
our fancy fire-places, which have contracted a
habit of smoking.

Last Wednesday we were again paid off.
This of course drew near the camp a long line
of passing wagons, which appeared like a
Hebrew funeral, old women with baskets and

boys with pails, all sorts of sharks selling to the soldiers very poor specimens of everything at very high prices. Some, however, send nearly all their wages home.   ALIQUIS.

November 13th, 1861, another letter from Camp Franklin to his brother is as follows :

"We are doing nothing much but drill and have no unusual excitement. Our commissions have just come and I am sorry to find that I'm not entitled to the place of Color-Captain, which I have been holding, and must go into the left wing. I find my commission dates fifth in order instead of third, as I had supposed. But it don't make much difference. Tom [his brother] and Captain Charley [a cousin] were over to see me about a week ago, and I since have made them a visit near Fort Corcoran. Tom is Commissary Sergeant—the same as ever, a favorite with all and with the privilege of going everywhere he pleases—says he is sure of a commission, etc., and is well and hearty—rides a splendid horse and gets up in style. Charley has the prospect of being a Major before long, he tells me. On my way over there I saw Jim Story, who is a Corporal and was sick in the hospital, and George Bowne, who seems to have grown a great deal. Tom lent me a cavalry horse to come back with."

Of course these extracts from private letters were never intended for publication, but after an elapse of thirty years I am sure they will be read with interest and gratification by his old friends and comrades.

THE CHAPLAIN ARRIVES.

DURING the summer the regiment was without any adequate religious aid or instruction, and it was not until the month of October, 1861, that their excellent chaplain, Rev. Dr. D. W. Bristol, received his appointment and went on to the regiment. His influence, it is stated, was most happy and beneficial. The following extract is from a letter of Dr. Bristol, dated November 22d, 1861 :

"Notwithstanding our difficulties, we have formed regimental church of some fifteen members. We lay aside our denominational peculiarities for the time being, and covenant to keep each other in the religious life. Several wanderers have returned to the great Master, and one, we trust, has been converted. We have also

organized a temperance society, which numbers,
I judge, somewhere about eighty members.   Our
beginning, we think, taking into account all the
circumstances, is a good one and encouraging."

A SOLDIER'S THANKSGIVING.

IN the following, Aliquis indicates why Generals Smith and Jones can enjoy a military review so much more than the men in the ranks, and then proceeds to draw upon his poetic imagination for a Thanksgiving dinner.

CAMP FRANKLIN, VA., November 24th, 1861.
To the Editor of the Utica Morning Herald:

Since I last wrote, I have been out on picket. This in cold weather is not so uncomfortable a duty as might at first be imagined, as nearly all the pickets are cantoned in deserted houses. Ours are nearly all stationed out at Annandale. where they are not much disturbed, except in their imaginations, perhaps, by some rebel artillery practising occasionally. On the day of the great review, last Wednesday, they kept up a

constant cannonading; with what object I know
not, perhaps by way of defiance. Our regiment
was sent out on picket duty then, because we
had "no new clothes to go to the show in;" for
Generals, you must know, like to see nice
parades, to revive, I suppose, the recollections
of boyish Fourths and "trainin's"; so I cannot
tell you much about the great review, but I shall
have to content myself with imagining. There
were innumerable white gloves, epaulettes and
brass buttons—the Generals were very dignified
and paternal—the mounted officers very serene
and fearless on their horses, spurring them forward on the ranks and then curbing them back-
ward on the brass bands—the line officers very
responsible and alarmingly straight in the back
—the men in the ranks tired and sullen, and the
brass bands very enduring to the end. The immense procession marched around the field, and
then Generals Smith and Jones saluted each
other and rode home, wondering, I suppose,
why the men never seem to enjoy these reviews.
. The Twenty-sixth, I suppose, will be allowed to
go to the next great parade, as we have just got
a splendid new suit of clothes, overcoats and
pants of dark blue cloth, and very neat forage
caps. You are already aware that we have
Sauer's brass band back again, which, with the
drum-corps, facetiously called "boiler-makers,"

furnish us with an abundance of music. Every
regiment in our brigade now has its brass band,
so that one may be heard playing nearly any
hour in the day.

Dr. Bristol, our Chaplain, is laboring assidu-
ously for the welfare of the men, and he has
formed a temperance organization, which is
gradually gaining in strength. It has been in-
correctly stated that Colonel Christian was the
President of this society. This was indeed
proffered him, but he declined accepting it, as
his military duties, he believed, would not allow him to take the leadership in any collat-
eral organization, though, of course, willing, as
much as possible, to promote the cause of temperance.

Well, the day is nigh at hand when the sov-
erign people of New York are to return thanks
to Divine Providence for the good digestive
organs with which they are gifted, and test
them accordingly. As this day approaches, I
am thereat much affected ; for in the poultry
line, I am conscious that they'll "miss me at
home, yes, they'll miss me." I assure you many
a Northern soldier thinks of his home in these
times ; of the old family gatherings ; the great
gastronomical exhibitions, concluding with a
grand display of molasses candy in the evening.

Oft in the stilly night,
    Ere slumber's chain hath bound me,
The thoughts of poultry bring the light
    Of other days around me—
Thanksgiving feasts of childhood's years,
    The words of cheer then spoken—
And then to think I'm penned up here,
    And all the hen-roosts played out long ago,
And my hopes of getting a furlough completely
    broken.

When I remember all
    The turkeys flocked together,
I've seen around me in the Fall,
    Up North, in just this weather,
I feel like one who treads alone
    Some dining-room deserted,
Whose lights are fled, whose garlands dead,
    And seein' he's got there too late,
Every darned joint of poultry has long since
    departed.

The Fifth Maine Regiment, whose camp adjoins ours, have just received twenty cases of turkeys from their native State, with which to do the honors of Thanksgiving day. I wouldn't like to be invited over there! Oh, no, not a bit of it. It ain't my style! (As Ward says, the above should be understood as irony.)

Many blankets have been received here lately from private sources, which have greatly increased the comfort of the men, and many a

grateful expression have I heard used when were
received the liberal contribution from the ladies
of Utica and Hamilton; quite a variety of clothing has been sent through me to men in this
regiment, for which thanks to all, the known
and the unknown.

More vigorous measures for the apprehension
of deserters are, I understand, to be now taken
by the government. Many are instigated to
desert by secessionists in Alexandria, some of
whom are now already ferreted out and arrested,
as I learn to-day. Some have decamped from
the Twenty-sixth since pay-day, and they will
be retaken, I suppose, if possible.

Money is very plentiful around Alexandria
and Washington, and peddling of all kinds is
very profitable. After a pay-day, when about
twenty-five or thirty thousand dollars is distributed through a regiment, it is astonishing to
see with what reckless freedom money is ex-
pended. Alexandria is now thronged with Jews
and Yankees vying with the native citizens as to
who shall carry off the greatest amount of army
gold. Fancy stores and saloons are continually
crowded, and finely dressed, polite gentlemen
are keeping lucrative "club-rooms," more accu-
rately, "gambling hells." Rabid secessionists
are fast getting wealthy off of the Union army,
and pocketing the new, hard gold with " 1861 "

stamped on it.   Still, I suppose, it can't be helped, while we remain here.   It is the universal wish that we may very soon go further south.   ALIQUIS.

A letter to his brother Stephen on January 11th, 1862, is addressed from Acquia Creek, Virginia. He writes: "I went out on another raid night before last and came back last night—about ten miles out.   Nothing important resulted from it, but the march back was the worst one I ever was on.   A cold rain was falling.   The road was mostly through the woods, and the soil of clay. The mud was knee-deep nearly all the way, and so dark no one man could see the other. I've just enough of the 'raid business' for the present.   We had a very dull holiday week. Your skating frolic would have been all I could ask for.   I, too, have had a letter from Tom. Soon as the Colonel gets back I shall make an effort to visit him.   He lies about ten miles from here.   Still in our comfortable quarters, with rumors of a move towards Warrenton, but nothing definite.   Sigel has returned, and we are all ready.   Where is the Twenty-ninth New Jersey?   I'd like to know where to find them."

A week later, from the same place, he again addresses his brother:

"No letter from home this week.   The Colonel

has returned, and I am relieved from much of my responsibilty. About a third of our line officers have been compelled to resign from disability, either mental or physical, so we're having a little revolution among us. To-night we're making an attempt to catch a 'secesh' that's aiding our men to desert. We have had about six desertions within a week. We've got a stool pigeon out to-night for him to practise on. We have been expecting to move daily for about a week, and we now expect to be ordered off to-morrow. In what direction no one knows. The weather is fine yet, and the nights beautiful. I occasionally pass my evenings with a family near here—a son, a major in secessia, but very pleasant. My love to all.   GEORGE."

FORT LYON.

O N February 5th, 1862, he is again back at
Fort Lyon. He writes: "I was employed
for twelve days as judge advocate on a general
court martial, which, by the way, is a very labor-
ious position. I, however, got $1.25 extra a day
while I was thus at work, and was relieved from
all other duty, which was the bright side of the
picture. We have had the 'allotment rules' in
circulation through the camp — I suppose you
have heard of them—and I have directed twenty-
five dollars a month of my pay hereafter to be
sent to father, and I hope generally to make
some additions by letter to this. I have not seen
George Bowne since I was home ; his company,
I learn, has gone over the river, and is—I do not
know where."

March 4th, 1862, he writes to Stephen from

Fort Lyon.   He states: "We have had some terrible hurricanes and a great deal of rain, which has made tent life rather disagreeable, but I have weathered it all and kept my health.   One of our company died about two weeks ago, the first since we have been in the service.   I had the body embalmed and sent home to Utica last week.   I haven't seen Tom in about a month, and he was well and happy then, and Charley was a major.   I don't think now there is much chance of being sent away, but everything seems to indicate a movement of some kind here.   Mc-Clellan's command now seems to be the only corps that is inactive, and I suppose its turn must soon come now.   We are now attached to Heintzelman's division.   We occasionally have some fine weather here now, but as a general thing high winds prevail.   These hurricanes, if they don't blow down our tents and leave us suddenly out-doors, always twist the stove-pipes around so, that fire is a nuisance, and cooking out of the question.   On such occasions we're obliged to eat 'what's left.'   About two weeks ago we had a gale which tore trees and overturned houses, and even baggage wagons, but I suppose we shall soon have some fine weather. Well, Stevey, write and tell me the news and don't wait for me.   If anything happens to me, or we make any movement, I shall write as soon as feasible."

Thus, beset by "hurricanes" and the lesser annoyances of "twisted stove-pipes," he consoles himself with the hope of finer weather in the future. One of Captain Arrowsmith's virtues was his happy disposition and cheerful contentment with his surroundings, let them be what they would. He was never finding fault with anybody or anything. If he had reason to believe that his company would be made the color company, or the first in rank, he still accepts it for the best when he finds it is otherwise ; though in politics of a party that is opposed to the war, no word escapes him disparaging to the government or its policy. Whatever may have been the shortcomings of a superior officer, and sometimes they were certainly conspicuous, he never refers to them. Though longing for an advance and the stirring events of an aggressive campaign, he is not impatient of inactivity. He is a true soldier, and accepts with philosophical equanimity every condition by which he is confronted.

On March 28th, 1862, he writes to his brother from Fort Lyon, Virginia :

" I suppose you have been anxious lately to know whether or not we have gone off on the expedition which embarked from Alexandria lately. You see by this, however, that I am in the same place, and may have to remain here yet some time. We are having splendid weather such as you have in May when you are planting, etc. To-day I took a long tramp over the country, but did not see much, though, but desolation. The New Jersey cavalry is yet near us, having been left to do scouting duty around the left flank of the army. I saw George Bowne last Sunday and he was looking very well and hearty. I am not able to ascertain whether Tom's regiment went off with the expedition or not, and havn't seen him in some time. I send enclosed a portrait of our Surgeon, a good friend of mine in the regiment. I am still well and hearty.

"Your affectionate brother,   GEORGE."

ALONG THE RAPPAHANNOCK.

A FTER a break of several months, he re-
sumes his letters to the *Utica Herald.*

CAMP RICKETTS, May 12th, 1862.

To the Editor of the Utica Morning Herald:

"Once more unto the breach, dear friends."
The only way I can justify the above quotation,
which I feel really conscientious about, is by re-
minding you of the great breach there has been
of late in the correspondence of your humble
servant, the undersigned. Our camp above-
mentioned is named after our present Brigadier-
General, and is not suggestive of any particular
disease prevailing in camp, as might at first appear.

After lying in a torpid state near Fort Lyon
all winter, we finally moved out of our haunts

about two weeks ago, and at present we infest the forests along the Rappahannock. The moving of the regiment infused new life into all; even the subscriber girded up his loins, paid some of his debts, disguised himself in a collar, and commenced the present letter.

The Twenty-sixth is at present in a brigade commanded by General James B. Ricketts, formerly captain of a regular battery which was captured at Bull Run, when its commander, above referred to, was wounded and taken prisoner. He is said to be a genuine fighting man. As we are the senior regiment of the brigade we occupy the right in line of battle. The regiments brigaded with us are the Ninety-fourth New York, the Eighty-eighth and Ninetieth Pennsylvania.

The greatest part of McDowell's army still lies on the Falmouth side of the river, one brigade only on the Fredericksburg side, though communication is free to and fro now by the pontoon bridge lately thrown across. The rebels have a force a short distance from the city, and still use the railroad that runs to Richmond. Fredericksburg is a city that presents quite an ancient appearance, as, indeed, it is an old town, having before the war some pretentions to business activity. The country around is finely adapted to raising corn and wheat, and immense fields of the latter are growing thriftily, unin-

jured by the army, as waste and marauding are
now the subject of very strict martial rules.
Except when the land, after being run out, has
been given over to scrub-oak and puny growth
of pines, the country here presents a beautiful
appearance—green plats sloping down towards
the Rappahannock, which rolls peacefully along,
with only the burned bridges and destroyed
shipping to remind us of the war. Over in the
city the places of business are mostly closed, and
it presents a sombre aspect, with little groups
of citizens lazily talking at the corners of the
streets, the omnipresent sentinel, and a few
ladies for whom you must step out into the
street, as chivalry and their crinoline seem to
entitle them to all the sidewalk.

You find one public-house open—the Planter's
Hotel—the proprietor of which is a very quiet
man, who never seems to meddle with either
politics or victuals, and the guest is annoyed
very little with either. Here you may get some
bacon, bread and butter, and tea, facetiously
called a dinner, for fifty cents : but you must
make your own change when you pay for it, or
you will receive in return perhaps a corporation
shinplaster, or a Confederate States of America
postage stamp, with a one-eyed picture of Jeff.
Davis on it. I think some visiting cards or railroad checks might make an excellent circulating

medium here now, for almost anything in the
shape of a bill will pass. Even the F. F. V.'s do
not have many of the luxuries of the table at
present. Whiskey is almost unknown in Fredericksburg, and appears only in saddened recollections. Bacon and corn bread are the articles
of food mostly in use here, with some tobacco
and a little abuse of the Northerners by way of
dessert. The political leaders around have told
me some pretty tough stories about us " Yankees," which I think they did not believe themselves. Sometime since I was seriously asked
by a lady in a rural district if the Yankee soldiers
really did make a practice of murdering the
children in the South, so as to eventually crush
the rebellion in this manner. Upon my informing her of the delight with which we participate
in the above refreshing diversion, I think she
really believed me, until my "silvery laugh"
gave her to understand that it was a "goak."
But the farmers here already begin to find that
a Northern army is not so bad a master after all.

The Southern pickets are stationed not far
from the city, and skirmishes with them are
of frequent occurrence, though it is generally
believed that no very large force lies in front of
us. What is proposed to be done with our corps
it is impossible to say, but I suppose we shall
push on soon. The railroad bridges between

here and Acquia Creek, that were burned by the
rebels on their retreat, are now nearly recon-
structed, and we shall soon have easy communication with Washington; and so we may expect
a rush of merchants to this place, bringing with
them all the benefits and evils of Northern en-
terprise.

Our regiment endured the winter with but
little loss. We have had some tiresome marches
since we came out of our quarters, yet our aggregate is yet eight hundred and forty men, which
is larger, I understand, than that of any other
New York regiment with the exception of the
Forty-fourth, alias the Ellsworth regiment. The
General this morning told the Colonel that we
might hold ourselves prepared to act as skir-
mishers at the first opportunity, so that altogether we are well satisfied with ourselves and
in the best of spirits. Were it not that compli-
ments paid to regiments were so stereotyped,
and belong peculiarly to the "mutual admiration society," I would repeat some paid us since
our arrival in this corps. We are at present
using the little shelter tents, which are trans-
ported from place to place on the backs of the
men ; but in this mild weather we are taking
the fortunes of campaigning quite comfortably.
Camp inconveniences have, however, obliged
me to violate a rule of press etiquette in the

form of my manuscript, which I beg you will excuse

Yours truly,   ALIQUIS.

CAMP RICKETTS, May 24th, 1862.
To the Editor of the Utica Morning Herald :

I fortunately have better conveniences for writing than I had when I sent you my last. I have mounted a steel pen *en barbette* on a pine stick, and am writing in a position which combines the posture of a Turk with the grace of the "What-is-it." We're having splendid weather now—cool and refreshing in the morning, but quite warm about noon, bringing out snakes of various sizes and hue, to bask along the edge of the roads where we are encamped. These unprincipled reptiles will sometimes even "vex the drowsy ear of night" with their rustlings among the leaves right around our tents. One of our officers, a few nights ago, was discovered in an undress uniform, making some very agile movements by a fire in front of his tent, in such a way that many supposed he was practising the "Indian War Dance." It was soon ascertained, however, that he was merely poking up a snake that had been sharing his hospitality, while he was asleep, by entering his tent and occupying a part of his blanket. Don't understand, for a moment, that we're afraid of

snakes. By no means; but then, such proceedings are unmilitary, to say the least, towards an
officer. Near this place is a stream called "Rat-
tlesnake Creek." I don't care (?) but then I wish
they'd give places more euphonious names.

All the country around here, if divided up in
smaller farms, and worked by some good Northern "mud-sills," could be brought under the
finest cultivation. As it is, some of it is very
productive, and will produce almost anything.
Adjoining our camp is a wheat field, containing,
I should think, about seventy-five acres. Its
rank growth is undisturbed by the soldiery, for
no one is allowed to walk through it, which certainly no soldier that had ever been a farmer's
boy could have the heart to do. Most of the
men who were left behind here, by the Southern
army, I think, are the "first families of Virginia"—that is, I think, they were the first men
that ever emigrated here, and have been here
ever since. Very few young, able-bodied men
are to be found, and these all have their stories
to relate of their perilous escapes from the
Southern cavalry.

About half a mile from our camp is General
Ricketts's headquarters—a fine mansion, with
its owner, a rank secessionist, still occupying a
part of it. A flag-staff and flag appear in the
yard now, to the evident disgust of the rebel

host, who lately called it a dishrag, in the hearing of a sentry there. It requires all the patience
that our men are possessed of to restrain from
acts of violence, when some protected traitor
thus speaks of the flag and cause for which
they are periling their lives. But, I suppose, it
is all for the best.

Mrs. Ricketts is still with her husband ; and
as she rides around the brigade with him, she is
vociferously cheered by the men, of whom she
is the idol. Her romantic journey to Richmond,
to join her husband in his painful imprisonment,
already belongs to history, and is the theme of
abler pens than mine. Her tale of the Richmond prisons, bringing to light the character of
many of the most prominent Southern generals
and Northern patriots, is of the most thrilling
interest, and throws far in the shade the narra-
tive of the Baroness Reidesel as a matter of historical romance. Soldiers of this corps, who
were then prisoners of war, are now frequently
seen at headquarters, returning thanks for her
kindness towards them in those hours of suffering ; and letters, expressive of gratitude, are
coming to her almost daily.

General Ricketts is now in command of a fine
brigade, who all hope, some day, to aid him to
enter Richmond in triumph.

General Shield's division arrived here last

night, very footsore and weary. Our corps is now complete, and we are expecting orders to march almost hourly, as we are held in constant readiness. Our division was paraded this afternoon before President Lincoln and Secretary Stanton, with the requisite amount of gilt, white gloves, music and cheering. The President was quite a curiosity to our secesh neighbors, who, I suppose, expected to see him in his shirt sleeves with an axe on his shoulders. We regard Lincoln's visit to this corps as the forerunner of an immediate advance.

Our division is commanded by General Ord, of Drainesville notoriety, an officer of high repute, who, it is said, will take the right of the corps in the advance. He rides a restless bay horse, which, like the famous cork-leg in the song, seems determined never to stop. This animal has a peculiar way of sideling up against fences and switching his tail in the faces of " the staff " and backing into the crowd, and making himself generally "around." Why am I so particular in describing this horse? Because you know an officer more by his horse than his "general orders," and I know of no better way of giving an impression of the nervous, grim, old Son of Mars who rides him.

Fredericksburg is beginning to look more lively. Mr. Hunt of New York, alias Farini,

the tight-rope walker, has opened the Shaks-
peare House, which, if I was a "penny-a-liner,"
I should say was so named because it was the
birthplace of the great English poet, but as it is,
I shall not venture it. Some fine stores are
opened, and the necessaries of life, beef, beer,
billiards, etc., are available. The railroad bridge
across the Rappahannock is guarded with the
greatest strictness, and the destruction of it
would be the cause of great delay. My next I
hope to write in a different camp.

ALIQUIS.

TALKS WITH PRISONERS.

A FORCED march from Fredericksburg in the hope of surprising Stonewall Jackson, brings the brigade to Front Royal, near the Shenandoah river, from which place comes the next letter.

FRONT ROYAL, VA., June 13th, 1862.

To the Editor of the Utica Morning Herald:

This morning we received a mail, for the first time in two weeks, and a very large mail it was, being escorted into camp in a baggage wagon. I went to work immediately to read my pile of papers, but have stopped in disgust as I got them mixed up somehow and found myself reading regimental autobiographies over three or four times, getting a vague idea that all the Oneida County volunteers had been killed, wounded or deified in McClellan's army. But all honor to the soldiers of Central New York. We received the record of their noble exploits in the late battles with a feeling of pride, and only regret that we could not have shared their fortunes in the grand army of McClellan.

Since I last wrote we have undergone some severe privations, though we have been guilty of no serious "breach of peace" under our sweet-tempered General McDowell. The prospect of entrapping Jackson sustained us on a forced march from Fredericksburg. At Front Royal we were much chagrined to find that we had arrived too late, and were booked for a bivouac in a cold rain storm, without either blankets, overcoats or tents. Worse than all, we in the advance crossed the Shenandoah and were cut off from our supplies by the destruction of both bridges, and the fierceness of the torrent prevented all intercourse; and still the rain kept falling, falling, for three days and nights, and yet scarcely anything to eat. However we not only fasted but preyed—upon the live stock in the vicinity, the excessive use of which has caused some sickness since. Finally the storm ceases, and after various experiments, resulting in the death of two men, a rope ferry is constructed, and we recross the river. It was "*sic transit*" however with many of us, though

a few days' rest since has brought the regiment
to its former state of health and buoyancy.

Our pickets took many of Jackson's stragglers
prisoners while over the river, with whom I had
a good opportunity to converse, as I had also
with those confined in the buildings in the village. They all pretend to be sanguine in the
belief that the confederacy is sure to succeed,
and that the Northern army can never entirely
conquer Virginia. They do not appear to claim
that the Southern soldier is in any way superior
to the Northerner, and the "one Confederate to
five Federal" idea, of which we heard so much
at the opening of the war, is entirely exploded.
They rely, however, on the dogged resolution to
fight to the last, their knowledge of the country
and the mountain roads, and their superior advantages for obtaining and giving information of
our movements which a war in their own country affords them. I am informed that the citizens boast of violating the oath of allegiance,
and regard it as a standing joke. Strange to
say, in their devotion to treason the men appear
not to "fear God" nor the ladies to "regard
man." The other day when I went to see the
captives in turn, I found numbers of ladies there
distributing food and bouquets among them,
and eyeing me askance with a malicious criti-
cism that made me feel much as I did years ago,

when I first went into company with a long-tailed
coat.   I was tempted to turn my coat wrong
side out, take a chew of tobacco, and pass for a
" secesh " myself ; but I didn't—the pie was all
distributed there, anyway.

I had quite a little political conversation with
one fellow, a complete gentleman, and of much
intelligence; yet even he had some odd ideas of
the North, and complained that the manufac-
tures and railroads and internal improvements
of the loyal States were the result of favor shown
them by the Federal government to the detri-
ment of the South.   I tried to undeceive him,
but unsatisfactorily to myself.   The fact is, the
" Union feeling in the South," and the deception
of the masses by the secession leaders are hardly
worth, I think, the attention that they elicit
from Northern politicians.   The bayonet is the
most successful persuader.   You remember when
we were school boys we could always perceive
much more clearly how naughty it was to play
truant after being soundly thrashed for it.

The wounded from two of Shield's Brigades
were brought into Front Royal to-day in a long
train of army wagons.   They present a pitiful
sight, but most of them will recover.   Though
jolted along over rough roads in these heavy
vehicles, hardly a groan ever escapes their lips,
and they bear their sufferings with the most

heroic fortitude. But do not believe all that you
read of rebel barbarities to wounded soldiers.
Those of the First Maryland Regiment that we
found quartered in houses around here tell no
such stories. In the heat of action, when the
brain is frenzied with the excitement of battle,
these are possibilities, but when the firing is
over, the soldier, in contemplating a wounded
enemy, is seldom governed by his ideas of State
rights or the Missouri compromise.

I wish we could always have as fine a mail as
that of to-day. I say unto you all, write. Anything in the form of a note is acceptable, and I
would even read a letter from Gerrit Smith or
Giddings, if it was addressed to me now. Our
friends—and creditors—must not wait for their
epistles to be always promptly answered, as
camp inconveniences often defeat our best in-
tentions. Not unfrequently our only means of
getting a letter to the office is through the "underground express," superintended by Richards,
the active correspondent of the *Telegraph*. All
ye who failed to "knit stockings" for the volunteers during the winter, redeem yourselves by
writing letters to them this summer.

ALIQUIS.

June 15th, 1862, writing from Centreville, Virginia, to his brother he says: "I am writing in

the Quartermaster's office, as we have formed
no regular camp, but are out in the field in the
sun. We have been on the move for three days,
marching about fifteen miles a day. It is very
warm, dusty and disagreeable. It seems a good
part of the army is coming here, and I expect
we shall have another Bull Run. We shall go
into it with good spirits at least, and God may
grant us a victory the third time, though the
enemy has doubtless the largest army again. I
am in command and would rather like a battle
in some respects under the circumstances. Still
it may run along so for weeks yet."

"The move for three days" above referred to
was from Front Royal to Centerville, a distance
of about forty-five miles. Captain Arrowsmith's
expectation of another battle of Bull Run in this
vicinity was very soon to be literally verified.

ASSISTANT ADJUTANT-GENERAL.

JUNE 25th, 1862, he writes from Manassas Junction, Virginia, to his father announcing an important event in his career, as follows: "I was chosen to-day by our new Brigadier-General Tower, to act as his Assistant Adjutant-General, and have been very busy with him all the evening. I have some prospects of being confirmed in the position, which I sincerely hope for, as it would increase my pay considerably, though not my rank, and also make me a mounted officer : but it's all uncertain yet. I am well and vigorous."

A few weeks afterwards, on August 19th, 1862, he received his commission, signed by Edwin M. Stanton, Secretary of War, with orders to report in person for orders to Brigadier-General Z. B. Tower.*

General Z. B. Tower was assigned to the command of the second brigade, second division, third corps, of the army of Virginia, about the last of June, 1862. General Ricketts, the division commander, recommended to General Tower, Captain Arrowsmith for the position of Assistant Adjutant-General, as an intelligent, educated, soldierly officer of good repute in his regiment, and the best-fitted person of his age in the brigade for this important place on the staff. Upon his appointment he became a permanent member of General Tower's military family, and his chief assistant. Having served since the beginning of the war, his experience was very valuable to him.

June 28th, 1862, installed in his new position, he writes his brother from Manassas Junction, Virginia :

"I have better conveniences for writing now, since I have been on the General's staff, as I have a large tent with a desk and a bed in it all to myself. As I mess with the General, who is quite an epicure, I live about as well now as I ever did in my life, and this eating with silver knives and forks scarcely seems like soldiering at

---

* Appendix, Note C.

all. However, when we get to marching it will not be so lovely again. I have a horse, etc., furnished by the government, and altogether I have a pretty comfortable time of it. I don't know how long I shall act in this capacity, but probably some time. I had a telegraph dispatch this afternoon from Tom, who wished to meet me in Washington this evening. It was impossible for me to comply with his request, as the most rigid orders are in force with reference to leaves of absence."   *   *   *   *

A SUMMER RESORT ENCAMPMENT.

ABOUT the middle of July Captain Arrowsmith is with his brigade at Warrenton,
near the Warrenton Springs, which we will learn
about in the next letter.

WARRENTON, VA., July 14th, 1862.

To the Editor of the Utica Morning Herald :

During the hot weather, and lately, we have
been sojourning at the celebrated summer resort
of Warrenton, occasionally taking a trip to the
Sulphur Springs for the sake of health. Warrenton is decidedly one of the finest towns I
ever saw, with fine mansions, flanked by lovely
gardens, and streets well shaded. This was a
favorite resort of Washingtonians in the warm
weather, and the register-book of the Warren
Green House would be a great treasure in the

eyes of an autograph collector. Like all other
watering places, Warrenton was remarkable for
the sparing manner in which the frequenters
thereof used water as a beverage. Here the Con-
gressional Representatives of Southern chivalry
used to assemble, and probably plot the destruction of the Union over chivalrous drinks of
whiskey. From this place did the gay visitors
start afternoons to go to the Springs to taste
some of the water, feeling, at the same time, with
remorse, that the habit of drinking water was
growing upon them, and winding its coils around
them. The favorite mode of getting to the
Springs was in an "extra" stage, driven by
one William Smith, who, in time, became better
known as "Extra Billy Smith," and drove himself not only into a fortune, but into a political
station. Then, when he got into the nice, big
house, with the double iron fence in front that
now graces Warrenton, the sobriquet stuck to
him still, as if saying to the traveler : "Billy
Smiths may be numerous: but here, sir, is something a little extra." Well, Billy is now in Richmond, helping to kill the Yankee invaders; but
in front of Billy's mansion in Warrenton may be
seen a sentry, in blue uniform, protecting Billy's
property from the inroads of the "mud-sills."
In view of the above service rendered, Billy's
wife and daughters tolerate the sentry.

General Tower has his headquarters at the residence of another Smith (ordinary quality), who is one of the editors of the Richmond *Enquirer*, and is quite generally known through Virginia. Among some old books and papers in the house, I find some sketches and descriptions of persons and places in the country, made during the travels of one Mrs. Anne Royall, who, notwithstanding the disregard which she constantly shows to religion and English grammar, gives some exceedingly minute descriptions. I am informed this female Willis once conducted a sort of paper in Washington, and treated the public to accurate descriptions of all celebrities. With those who patronized her "all the men were brave, and all the women were beautiful:" but, alas, for those who refused to yield to the blackmail imposed. Among the families mentioned in Warrenton by Mrs. Royall is that of the Lee, which being descended neither from Pocahontas nor Washington, is, of course, in the lineal stock of "Light Horse Harry" of the Revolution. The female who now supports the dignity of the Lee family owns a farm which supplies the soldiers with much fruit and forage. Altogether, this is a fine country and provender is abundant; but I could have forgiven the natives for a great deal of their treasonable conduct, if they had only left a little larger supply of ice for us.

The Warren Green Hotel in the town is now taken for a hospital, for which it is finely adapted, and will afford good accommodations for the sick of the whole army here. This is a step in the right direction, for so far from being of any sanitary use before being taken, there had not been a bar properly kept in it for months. The regiments around here are in good state generally speaking as regards health, the Twenty-sixth New York especially. After a march, or a change of location and water, a great many will always be a little unwell, but no serious epidemics are prevailing. Major Jennings has been quite unwell for the last few days, but is steadily recovering.

Our mails still come in a very irregular manner, but I assure you they are eagerly received. There seems but very little system and certainty in the matter, and I would caution all those who are indebted to me to refrain from sending money to me in any very large sum through this medium. A breach of this rigid rule might occasion it to come into the hands of some unprincipled robber who would squander it in an unprofitable manner.

We quite frequently see Richmond papers in town, and it is strongly suspected that a regular mail is received and sent here. It is possible it may be so, as there has been no severity shown as yet by the government towards spies, and they run but little risk. This is really the most civil war ever heard of. Out at Front Royal, Bell Boyd boasts and jokes of her participation in Colonel Kennedy's defeat in the very face of the Generals, and laughs pleasantly at the idea of being arrested. To check this system of espionage some one should be hung—some *guilty* person should be the example if possible; but one thing is certain, some one should be pendant for the good of the Union.

I have just received, by the way, the Utica papers, and get much more warlike enthusiasm from reading of the determination of Central New York to send still more troops into the service than in witnessing the dull routine of this army of occupation. It seems as though the strong and persevering effort made in Utica can not be a failure, with such a man proposed for commander as Captain Pease.

No man can be without the gratitude of his fellows that volunteers at the present crisis. In the army now in the field doubtless some have enlisted for ambition, for adventure, for money, some perhaps because they didn't get married when they wanted to, and some because they did; but the great novelty of the war is now

over, and no one can doubt, I think, the motives
of those who will meet the last earnest call for
troops, to fill up the gaps in the army made by
disease and by the bullet.

I know not what will be done with us here,
but suppose we shall push on towards Gordons-
ville.   Generals Banks and Sigel were both in
Warrenton a few nights ago.   McDowell I have
not seen for weeks, and I guess that it is only
at "Willard's" that he is visible to the naked
eye.   Nor has Pope yet made his appearance.
General Ricketts and General Tower are, however, constantly with their commands, and hard
at work keeping everything in readiness for
marching orders.   One hundred and forty rounds
of cartridges are always kept on hand, and the
baggage trains in order, but still we are *in statu
quo*, and I might add *ante bellum*.

ALIQUIS.

NEW DUTIES.

FROM Waterloo, Virginia, August 4th, 1862, in a letter to his brother Stephen, he writes :

"I believe I must tell you something of the life and duties of an Assistant Adjutant-General (an awkward title, by the way). Well, I have to issue and keep on file all general and special orders and circulars, transact all the business correspondence of the General and keep on file all letters received and sent, make out all the weekly and monthly returns of the brigade, make all details, keep the countersigns and signals in my possession and issue them daily on the field, act as *aid-de-camp* to the General, transmit orders and direct the columns. Three or four hours' work in the day, though, generally does all my business, though it's quite confining. I have bought a magnificent horse, for which I've paid what will appear a pretty steep price to you, two hundred dollars. However, I would not sell him for that now. He is a large sorrel horse, rather showy, a good jumper, eight years old and sound. I've now had him about a month. By the way, I have a clerk allowed me, and an orderly to take care of my horse, besides my waiter, whom (the latter) I have to pay myself, as usual. So I've told you now pretty much all about my present *status*. I was offered, not long since, a lieutenant-colonelcy in one of the New York regiments, that has not yet scarcely begun to make any show, but I refused it, as I saw they would expect me to work about and spend money for the rest; and then, I reflected, that being green the regiment would always be kept in the background, which I'm tired of. I'm well, have plenty to eat, and generally a good place to sleep, which is saying considerable for a soldier. I wish I could be home awhile in the market season, though. We move in the night, I'm told. Good night!"

"P. S.—Marching orders come."

CEDAR MOUNTAIN.

THE battle of Cedar Mountain was fought on the ninth of August, 1862. It was Banks against Ewell, each with about eight thousand men. For awhile the fight was in favor of the national troops, but rebel reinforcements coming up, Banks retreated before the enemy. Pope was only a few miles away; he hurried up and checked the pursuit. Arrowsmith was with Ricketts's division of Pope's forces. His brigade saw the main part of the fight, but was engaged only in the last of it. Captain Arrowsmith acquitted himself so well as to earn favor from General Tower. He thus speaks of the battle in a letter to his brother from Mitchell Station, dated August 17th, 1862: "Our brigade was not in the main part of the fight at all, though we had a good sight of it. We were on the

right of Ricketts's division, which you know
came up in time to check the rebels after they
had begun to drive Banks. When we came on
the ground, Banks's exhausted troops passed to
the rear of us and all was quiet for some time.
About midnight they came up about two or three
hundred yards from us and commenced shelling
us. Two of our batteries commenced at them
so sharply that in about half an hour they completely silenced them, having killed nearly all
their horses and made great havoc generally.
This was all of the fight that we were really in.
Our division lost one hundred and six, killed and
wounded. Since the battle General Tower has
nominated me to the Secretary of War for con-
firmation in my position, at which I am much
delighted. No time to write more. Good-by ! ''

SECOND BULL RUN.

ENGAGEMENTS at Rappahannock, Thoroughfare Gap and Second Bull Run (or Groveton) quickly followed. The two former were essentially artillery engagements. In the last-named battle Captain Arrowsmith was in the thickest of the fight, and regardless of danger, discharged his duties with great efficiency. His brigade was the first thrown into the action by General Ricketts. General Tower was in command and led the advance. Fairly enveloped by the advancing enemy, the loss of men was very severe, infantry upon three sides of them pouring in its deadly volleys, and artillery firing upon them from a hill close by. Captain Arrowsmith's duties covered a large area, transmitting orders from one point to another, and directing columns. His slouch hat, straight

black hair, swarthy face and erect figure made
him a conspicuous object, dashing on horseback
in every direction, inspiring by his example the
courage of the Union soldiers and a target for
the enemy's sharpshooters. General Tower fell
wounded seriously while gallantly leading his
brigade. "Captain George Arrowsmith," wrote
a correspondent of the New York *Tribune*, "formerly of the Twenty-sixth New York, but promoted by General Tower as Assistant Adjutant-
General of his brigade for gallantry, showed
great bravery on the field. His praise is in the
mouth of every one. At one time he is said to
have taken General Schenck for a major, and immediately rode up and led two regiments into
the fight, amid a shower of grape and canister."
Fessendon, a brother officer on General Tower's
staff, was killed. The loss of the brigade was
terribly severe. Captain Arrowsmith's escape
without a wound was almost miraculous. One
bullet passed through his hair, another struck his
sword scabbard, and a third had buried itself in
the folds of his blanket, which he discovered at
the close of the fight. It was here he won for
himself the sobriquet of "the young lion." A
hastily written letter to his father dated September 1st, 1862, from Centreville, Virginia, briefly
refers to the battle. "Our brigade got into a
terrible fight in the battle of the day before yes-

terday. We found ourselves in a trap where
there was infantry on three sides and artillery
firing on us from a hill. The brigade has lost between five hundred and one thousand men. I
write this to inform you that I'm not hurt. General Tower was wounded and was sent to Washington yesterday. Fessendon, of the staff, was
shot dead. The closest shave I made was a bullet through my hair, though one hit my sword
scabbard, and when I lay down for the night, a
ball dropped out of my blanket, that I had kept
folded on the front of my saddle. Will never
get in a worse place. Very busy."

After three weeks of almost incessant fighting
with the army of General Pope, marching and
countermarching from Cedar Mountain back
across the Rappahannock, thence to Thoroughfare Gap, thence to Manassas ; back to Centreville, and thence to Chantilly, where the gallant Kearney of New Jersey fell, his physical
powers were reduced to a degree that he was
unable to withstand a shock sustained by a fall
of his horse, and upon the recommendation of
General Tower, who lay seriously wounded in
Washington, he accepted a leave of absence for
the purpose of recruiting his weakened frame.

The following is the letter of General Tower,
requesting a furlough for Captain Arrowsmith :

WASHINGTON, September 15th, 1862. .

To General Cullom :

If you can do so consistently I wish you would give my Adjutant-General a leave to go home. I have no doubt that it will hasten his recovery and return to duty. He is an officer of the true stamp and mettle and will doubtless return the instant he is able to resume his duties. For the past two months he has continued on duty when most officers would have reported sick, and has done active field duty when it was very painful for him to sit upon his horse, so anxious was he to be at his post of duty and danger. Now it is best that he should try to effect his recovery before the injury becomes more difficult to cure. I therefore ask this indulgence for him.

With respect, your most obedient,

Z. B. TOWER,
Brig. Gen. Bvt.

Owing to his wounds, General Tower was compelled to give up the command of the Second Brigade, which ended Captain Arrowsmith's service upon his staff.

Under date of September 4th, 1862, we find Captain Arrowsmith at Brown's Hotel in Washington, from which place he addresses his brother Stephen, as follows : "I wrote a day or two ago informing you that I was safe, but as I had to

send it by the 'underground railroad,' to avoid
Halleck's order, I feared lest possibly it might
be intercepted. I have been in the battles of
Rappahannock, Thoroughfare Gap, and Saturday's battle of Bull Run. In the latter our brigade, through a blunder, was badly cut to pieces.
General Tower was badly wounded, and is now
at Willard's. Fessendon was killed. I escaped
unhurt, but was reported to be killed, and my
Washington friends are all much surprised to
see me. I woke up the morning after the fight
and found myself quite a hero on a small scale.
Colonel Christian did not go into the fight.
Poor Leonard, second lieutenant of my old company, was shot dead. Our brigade is now over
the other side of Munsen's hill, about five miles
from Washington. I am staying in Washington
a day or two by the doctor's advice, to cure up a
slight injury I received from my horse falling on
me during the battle. Tell me, are you drafted?
Tom is well. I have had no mail for about two
weeks, and I have a lot of letters somewhere, I
expect. When I came into town this morning,
I had not changed my clothes in three weeks,
and was as ragged and dirty as a beggar. Fortunately, I had money enough to make a trans-
formation. My love to all."

TRIBUTE FROM GENERAL TOWER.

GENERAL TOWER is still living, residing at Cohassett, Mass., and in a kindly letter of recent date to Stephen V. Arrowsmith, he thus refers to the service of Captain Arrowsmith upon his staff : "During the two months that the brigade was under my command, whether in camp, on the march or engaged in battle, Captain Arrowsmith, with professional pride and untiring devotion, met all the requirements of his position as Assistant Adjutant-General, to my entire satisfaction. Now, after the lapse of so many years, I am glad to have the opportunity to bear testimony to his marked soldierly qualities, his coolness, self-command and gallantry of action, which made him one of the most promising of the young officers of my command. General Pope's campaign involved

the advance of his army to the Rapidan in the
vicinity of which, after the battle of Cedar
Mountain, its several corps were concentrated—
the subsequent falling back north of the Rappahannock before General Lee's advance—holding
that river as a line of defence beyond Waterloo
bridge for many days, thus delaying the enemy's
progress and giving time for a portion of the
Peninsula forces to unite with General Pope's
army—the affairs of Bristoe Station and Thoroughfare Gap, the battles of August 29th and
30th at Groveton, and the partial engagement
of September 1st at Chantilly — the last two
weeks of this campaign, with its marches and
countermarches by day and night, through rain
and over mud roads, or under the intense heat of
an August sun, in a malarious district and with
frequent conflicts with the enemy, were a severe
test of the physical endurance of the command
and rapidly diminished its numbers by exhaustion and disease, incident to overwork and exposure.   Such a campaign might well shake the
resolution of soldiers, unaccustomed by long service to like hardships, so that those who stood
bravely to their colors from the beginning to the
end of the campaign, deserve and should receive
the highest commendation for their fortitude and
courage, though they were eventually forced

back, overmatched by an enemy elated by recent
successes on another field.

"It is my recollection that Captain Arrowsmith throughout these trying services never
yielded to overwork of any kind, and was never
absent for a day from his post of duty, but was
actively efficient unto the end, and on every battle field he evinced the cool gallantry to which
I have already given my testimony.

"Having been severely wounded in the battle
of August 30th, I was compelled to give up the
command of the Second Brigade and part with
my staff officers, to whom I had become much
attached during their short but eventful service
and association with me. Not one of those
three officers who were so constantly by my side
during the campaign, and all sat at the same
table with me, survived the war. The brigade
sergeant, Abraham Cox, died at Lookout Mountain; Lieutenant Samuel Fessendon, my aid, a
gallant youth, fell mortally wounded in the battle of Groveton; and your brother, having served
on many battle fields, was killed at Gettysburg.
I heard of his death with pain and sorrow, for
he was a valued friend, a man of worth and a
sterling soldier. I am, very truly yours,

"Z. B TOWER,
"*Bvt. Maj. Gen'l, U. S. Army.*"

LIEUTENANT-COLONEL.

IN JUNE, 1862, Melville D. Landon (Eli Perkins), a Washington correspondent of the press, wrote to State Senator John J. Foote, a leading Republican of Hamilton, New York, suggesting Captain Arrowsmith for promotion to a field office in a New York regiment then about to be organized. Just prior to the outbreak of the rebellion Senator Foote's mind had not been free from prejudice toward Arrowsmith, due perhaps to his youthful partisanship as manifested by racy communications to the local Democratic paper ; but these prejudices, Senator Foote acknowledged in his reply to Mr. Landon, were dispelled by Arrowsmith's manly and patriotic course at the outbreak of the war, when he came out boldly for his country and enlisted in its service, while very many of his

party were semi-secessionists. This letter is replete with the evidences of kind feeling. It
states that Captain Arrowsmith "is a good officer in every respect," "a brave and loyal man."
"You may do as you think best in regard to expressing to him my opinion. If I can help him
at any time it will afford me great pleasure to
do so, for two reasons. The first because I consider him worthy, and secondly, because it
would afford me an opportunity to demonstrate
my regard for him." This letter was forwarded
by Mr. Landon to Captain Arrowsmith, with a
request that he write to Senator Foote. Captain Arrowsmith did so and there followed correspondence between them which shows that
notwithstanding past differences, Senator Foote
had come to entertain towards Captain Arrowsmith a very kindly feeling and a high regard.
The Senator answers him that he is very grateful for the opportunity offered for mutual ex-
planations, and adds : "If my feeling of dis-
like for you had not been dissipated while we
were at Mr. Greenley's (a boarding-house at
Hamilton), your noble course at the breaking
out of the war was such as would have dispelled
all such feelings. I take pride in the fact that I
was first to suggest you for captain, and I have
never seen reason to regret it. You at once
rose *above party feeling* that existed at that time,

and consecrated yourself to the service of your
country, and ever since I have been anxious for
your promotion." Senator Foote then refers to
the fact that a movement has commenced in his
senatorial district, comprising the counties of
Madison and Cortland, for the organization of
a regiment to help make up the new levy, and
that he had suggested his name for Colonel or
Lieutenant-Colonel ; and he adds : "It takes
well, but there is a difficulty to be encountered.
Professor Brown, of Madison University, wants
a position as a field officer, and it would be impossible to get a place for both, as both would
be regarded as hailing from Hamilton." Professor Brown was a brilliant scholar, well known
in Madison county and had many friends ; he
was a man of energetic character, full of patriotic zeal, and had devoted himself industriously
to the work of soliciting recruits for the new
regiment, addressing public meetings every
night throughout the district. He was principal of the Grammar School connected with the
University, and Arrowsmith had been associated
with him, first as pupil and then as his assistant.
Their personal relations were of the most friendly character and there could be no rivalry between them There was mutual correspondence,
which resulted in Captain Arrowsmith positive-
ly refusing to accept the colonelcy of a regi-

ment over Brown, his old friend and his senior
in years.   By the latter part of August, Brown
had succeeded in enlisting eight hundred men
for his regiment, and his appointment to the
Colonelcy was assured.   There was much rivalry
between the counties comprising the district for
the honor of filling the other regimental offices.
Senator Foote was one of the State Senatorial
Committee for the organization of regiments in
his district, which gave him considerable influence both at home and with Governor Morgan,
who was the appointing power.   He arranged a
plan by which the objection to appointing the
two highest regimental officers from the same
place lost its force.   This plan contemplated re-
serving the office of Lieutenant-Colonel to be
filled by a man of experience from the army.
Then, instead of dividing the other regimental
offices equally between Madison and Cortland
Counties, he would magnanimously grant to
Cortland whatever it asked.   With this arrangement in view, an invitation was extended to the
committee from Cortland County to meet Senator Foote at his office in Hamilton the evening
of August 23d, 1862.   Judge Mason and Professor Brown were also present by invitation.
The proposition was made by Senator Foote in
accordance with the plan stated.   It was har-
moniously accepted.   The office of Lieutenant-

Colonel was to be left vacant and to be filled from the army. This being settled, Senator Foote then presented the name of Captain Arrowsmith as an experienced officer in the army, and a native and resident of New Jersey, although a graduate of Madison University and a law student with Judge Mason in Hamilton up to the time of his enlistment. Senator Foote wrote, " It took first-rate." He then called on Judge Mason for an expression of his views, which the Judge of course fully gave, accompanied by a reading of recommendations from the army. Colonel Brown was on hand, who heartily seconded the proposition.

Thus, by the direction of Senator Foote, it was fully arranged to organize the One Hundred and Fifty-seventh Regiment, New York State Volunteers, with a vacancy in the office of Lieutenant-Colonel, and with the understanding that an invitation was then to be given to Captain Arrowsmith to accept the position. There were some underhanded attempts afterwards at Albany to get another person appointed, but this was readily defeated by Senator Foote and Judge Mason through Governor Morgan.

As soon as it was known that Captain Arrowsmith was to be the Lieutenant-Colonel and Professor Brown the Colonel, there was much dissatisfaction expressed in the district because

Arrowsmith could not be Colonel. There was the highest respect for both, but Arrowsmith had earned a reputation in the field while Brown was inexperienced. Senator Foote writing to Captain Arrowsmith stated that he "saw Governor Morgan and he would have given you a commission as Colonel of the regiment if I had said so, but you were not here to consult and so I did not say the word." Judge Mason in a letter written to Captain Arrowsmith's father stated, " He should have been appointed the Colonel, and so Governor Morgan said, after he read the high testimonials from the army, but George was in the field and the regiment was half filled, and they must have a Colonel then."*

Senator Foote now, under date of September 22d, 1862, wrote to Captain Arrowsmith telling him all that had been done, and urging him to accept the position. Arrowsmith had previously written him referring to the order of the War Department forbidding army officers leaving their positions for the purpose of accepting offices in new regiments. Senator Foote wrote. in reply: "I was aware of this and so was Governor Morgan, and he mentioned it as an objection, but we pressed you over that, believing you would manage some way to get excused

---

* Appendix, Note D.

so as to accept the place. We thought that if they would not allow you to leave the field now, that you would be allowed to do so as soon as this regiment got away and in the army. The fact is, we have not allowed any obstacle to get into your way. Now I hope you will not relinquish the idea of accepting this post."

Events show that he did accept it, though he was being urged about the same time for the colonelcy of the Twenty-sixth New York Volunteers, in place of Colonel Christian, who had resigned. Adjutant Bacon was one of his earnest advocates for the last-named place ; and Governor Parker of New Jersey, urged by prominent citizens of that State, had given assurances that' he would appoint him to the colonelcy of a New Jersey regiment when a favorable opportunity offered.

Enough is written to show that the Lieutenant-Colonelcy came to Captain Arrowsmith upon the merit of his reputation as a man and a soldier, without his leaving the field, and without an effort in his own behalf. He was commissioned by Governor Morgan of New York, September 16th, 1862, with rank from August 23d, 1862.

On the twenty-fifth of September the One Hundred and Fifty-seventh Regiment left New York for its encampment at Centreville, Virginia, near Washington.

On the twenty-sixth of October following, we find Lieutenant-Colonel Arrowsmith at Washington, where he is waiting for the acceptance of his resignation as Assistant Adjutant-General, almost well and quite anxious to get out with the regiment. "Adjutant Bacon," he writes, "has returned from Utica and is here at Brown's Hotel. He says his father is urging my claims with Governor Morgan as Colonel of the Twenty-sixth, though I'm quite indifferent whether he succeeds or not, as the regiment's time will be out next May."

November 3d, 1862, George writes his brother Stephen from Washington. * * * * "I find my regiment has got up to their ears among the Dutchmen, in Sigel's corps, Carl Schurtz's division, and Colonel Schimmelfenning's (or some such name) brigade. I don't particularly fancy this arrangement altogether. I havn't seen the Twenty-ninth yet, as it requires quite a long horseback ride to do it."

The One Hundred and Fifty-seventh Regiment appears to have been the only "Yankee Regiment," as it was called, in the division, the entire corps being largely made up of Germans and known as the German corps. It was a peculiar position. An American regiment serving its country in a German army. If it achieved victory, to the Germans belonged the glory. If

it suffered defeat there was precious little consolation in the thought that the shame was the
Germans. If George was not particularly
pleased with this assignment of his regiment, as
several sportive references to the matter in his
correspondence would seem to indicate, it was
perfectly natural. But he found no fault with
it. He accepted the situation as one of the acci-
dents of war, and here as elsewhere he knew
only his duty as a soldier.

A PLEASING RECEPTION.

LIEUTENANT-COLONEL Arrowsmith had not yet seen the regiment of which he was Lieutenant-Colonel. It had now been in camp nearly two months, and there began to be a good deal of anxiety manifested as to when their Lieutenant-Colonel was coming, and what he was like. They knew him by reputation as a man who had had experience in the army and had been under fire. This was more than could be said of anybody else in the regiment, and of course there was curiosity to meet him and have him with them. About the middle of November he joined the regiment at New Baltimore.

A writer in the Canastota *Herald* of the date of July 18th, 1875, thus describes the impression made by the young officer as he approached the regiment for the first time : " What a scanning that young, black-eyed, black-haired officer in slouched hat received as he came down the hill at New Baltimore to attend the dress parade. It was early in November, when the pinching frosts and chilling winds of Dixey were telling in dampening effect upon the mirth and romance of camp life. 'Is that our Lieutenant-Colonel?' says one, after the parade was dismissed. 'He does look like a bully boy,' says another. 'See that long cavalry sword he carries : that looks as though it had seen service,' remarks another. And so was Colonel Arrowsmith discussed, but always with a decided bias in his favor. For who could see aught but welcome in his pleasant face, and deny him the same welcome from a thousand hearts.

"It was at once apparent to the eyes of his men that Colonel Brown had found in Colonel Arrowsmith a counsellor as well as a companion in arms ; while Colonel Arrowsmith, from his long experience in active service, seemed to reciprocate such consideration by becoming modesty towards his superior. The men, too, soon found that instead of another 'high dig' to lift their hats to simply, a man had come who sought only their best interests and advancement in the ways of a soldier, for he seemed to feel that his surest way to honor lay in a proper attention to the general welfare of the men of his regiment. On the march, if he held the command, he sought the easiest part of the road, found the best water and the coolest shade possible for them ; when a sharp bend in the route occurred he cut across lots to save distance, and rested just as long and often as allowed by his superiors. Who could not like such a man ? In camp, when on drill under the Lieutenant-Colonel, the men under such guidance moved with vigor and alacrity, and in excellent trim returned to their quarters thankful for the experience and skill of such an able officer."

November 16th, 1862, he writes to his brother Stephen : *   *   *   * "I've rather enjoyed starting campaigning again, so far. General Schurtz seems to be a very fine, affable man, and hardly a foreigner, but our brigade commander is Dutch enough for all practical purposes. Our regiment is under excellent discipline and my associates very pleasant, gentlemanly fellows. So I start again in very good spirits for another campaign. *   *   *   * We are ordered to march in the morning, but I don't know in what direction, but I think the movement inclines towards Fredericksburg. I find it is much easier to be Lieutenant-Colonel than it was on the staff, as then I had nearly everything to do, now almost nothing. We are having beautiful autumn weather, with a fine bracing air, just right for military operations. I find myself pretty well acquainted with the country, and enjoy visiting the scenes of my old hardships and battles."

WASHINGTON IN 1862.

UNDER date of November 24th, 1862, Aliquis
addresses the Utica *Herald* from Centreville, Virginia, which is his last letter to that
journal, affording us a glimpse of the metropolis
in the days of the Rebellion.

CENTREVILLE, VA., November 24th.

To the Editor of the Utica Morning Herald:

A few days since I saw in some journal that
the Utica *Herald*, on account of the increased
expense of publishing newspapers, had been reduced in size. I noticed since, however, that
your paper has risen, like the Phœnix from its
own ashes, and appears as a fine, double sheet.
Blessed be newspapers ! No matter if the news
items do sometimes draw very heavily upon the
imagination. " We pays our money and we takes

our choice," should be our consolation, when we
are at a loss which to consider as miscellany,
Sylvanus Cobb's tale, or the telegraphic column.

I am now in Sigel's Corps, Schurtz's Division,
and Schimmelfenning's Brigade. The names,
you perceive, are all Italian and " breathe of the
sweet South." We have been solemnly informed
through the Washington papers several times
that we have been cut to pieces and driven back to
Alexandria, but in the language of the lamented
Webster, " we ain't dead yet," having seen nothing calculated to produce death, with the exception of commissary's whiskey, since I have been
here.

We have been marching and countermarching
about this part of Virginia for a few days, I
suppose for the purpose of covering the recent
movement towards Fredericksburg. By a recent order, Sigel's Corps is made the reserve
of the grand army, whose duty I presume it will
be to protect a place called Washington, the
guarding of which has caused nearly every
movement of our armies to miscarry, and has
cost the country much more than it was ever
worth. I will give you a description of it.

The city of Washington, aside from the public
buildings, consists of four hotels, Pennsylvania
Avenue, Grover's Theater, and Gautier's saloon.
The rest of the place is a succession of country

villages, with low, illy-planned houses, with
small negroes leaning on the piazzas. It is a
capital place to spend a fortune, being abun-
dantly supplied with extortioners, hackmen, bar-
keepers and Jews. The best places to get rid of
money are Joe Hall's gambling saloon and Willard's Hotel, though these places have many as-
piring rivals. There are no particular social
distinctions in Washington, but there is a sort
of barber-shop and bar-room sociability in which
every one who wears good clothes may participate. You hardly ever meet any one who is an
actual resident of Washington. These crowds
that you meet are all men away from home, and
hence unsettled, anxious, reckless, seeking for
positions, for contracts, for a living without
working, for the necessary bread without the
usual amount of perspiration required in the an-
tediluvian sentence. You must not be surprised
at meeting any old acquaintance in Washington.
Your friend Jones or Smith, who greets you so
cordially around home, shakes hands with you
as a matter of course in Washington, but he ex-
cuses himself and hurries on, as he is expecting
to meet some one of more influence at the Departments. No one is interested in what does
not concern himself, and sensations and riots
are uncommon. When it was expected the city
would be taken by the confederates, there was

no great concern, the billiard balls were clicking
all day, and the theatres crowded at night.
From nine o'clock in the morning till three
o'clock in the afternoon crowds are jostling
around the Departments, the offensive party.
The defensive is sustained by cool, indifferent
clerks and ushers. Business is business with
them, and unless the applicant claims relation-
ship with some one in the establishment he is
conscientiously excluded.

The rural visitor in the city, if he has not before been accustomed to this mixed society of
clerks, gamblers, officers, fortune hunters and
Congressmen, seems relieved by a breath of
fresh, home air again, when he returns from this
city, Washington, the Political Metropolis, and
ex-officio the Metropolis of Corruption.

So much for the city of magnificent distances.
But still " I'd have no objections to seeing it a
little longer," as the culprit on the scaffold replied to the priest when told that " life was all
a fleeting show." Centreville is about as desolate a looking place as can well be imagined,
and the country having been crossed and re-
crossed by armies on both sides, every available
field has before been occupied as a camping
ground. The usual traces of an army are visible
on all sides ; all sorts of filth and garbage, in
which fevers are lurking ; recumbent horses,

very fat and plump, but on the whole, looking as though they might be dead or something of that sort. No serious epidemics are as yet prevailing, however, yet it is to be hoped that our winter quarters will not be taken at this place. Notwithstanding what is felt and said on the subject of a winter campaign, it is evident to all who have had any military experience in this climate, that if Richmond is not taken within a month, the state of the roads will check all active operations in the field. With Richmond as a new base it might be different, but from our present base it requires a pretty energetic General to give an army three meals a day at the best of times and under the most favorable circumstances.

I have not seen the Twenty-sixth in some time. By some of your army correspondence, I notice their chaplain has again joined them. The splendid body of men that languished in *otium cum dignitate* at Fort Lyon one year ago, speculating on the chances of seeing active service, has in a series of campaigns been transformed into a small band of veterans. As the old organizations dwindle and disappear in the discharge of their duty, new ones are rushing in to fill their places, to have, I suppose, the same experience. ALIQUIS.

A REMINISCENT LETTER.

THE Lieutenant-Colonel being now installed in his new position, addresses the writer the following reminiscent letter :

CENTREVILLE, VIRGINIA, Nov. 28th, 1862.

Dear Chum :

In camp, near Centreville, very comfortable tent. Pleasant though cool weather. Regiment out firing at a target. I'm lonely and rather blue ; my horse has got the hoof-rot, and cannot be used. I am a little unwell yet and off duty; I am out of reading matter and must write letters. In commencing a letter to you, old times come up before me. What strange things a few years bring to pass ! The Brown that we used to designate as " Long Brown " in distinction from other Browns of no less marked

peculiarities, is Colonel of a regiment, and I
Lieutenant-Colonel. An old Madison student,
Day; the ex-editor of the *Republican*, Waldron ;
and Judd Powers, are privates in the regiment.
Sam Wickwire, formerly known as "Gumbo,"
is a Second Lieutenant. Last summer when on
the staff I was visited by a Sergeant, who turned
out to be Palmer, who graduated when I did—
he that of old first tasted of war in an encounter
with George Eaton, one night when the "rust
was rung" at Madison. Ford, of your class,
was a Commanding Sergeant in my brigade last
summer. The other day I met Moses H. Bliss,
D. K. E., a private in the Forty-fourth New
York Volunteers. MacIntyre, Curtis, and Mrs.
Haskell's sons are dead. Carl Schurtz, the orator, is our General here, and other Dutchmen of
whom we probably bought lager beer three
years ago, are my compeers in other regiments.
War, like misery, makes strange bedfellows; as
you remarked in one of your productions of
yore, "a bundle of negations and inconsist-
encies." Our lines have truly fallen in Dutch
places, we being the only Yankee regiment in
the Division. "Yankee," I suppose by the way,
should have its usual prefix, D—n Yankee.
Custom has made it all one word among our
secesh opponents, "Damnedyankees." I like
General Schurtz very well, though I am not so

enthusiastic over our Brigadier Schimmelfenning, whose name, as Ward would say, is "pyure
Spanish." But, *per contra*, as the Dutch always
look out for enough food to eat, and whiskey
to drink, we are well taken care of, and "fare
sumptuously every day on purple and fine
linen," which is a quotation, sir, a quotation!
I find that P. P. makes a first-rate Colonel, and
is very pleasant to be associated with. Even
war produces some change in him! He does
not swear yet, but occasionally says he wants to,
and drinks nothing as yet stronger than wine,
but he smokes excessively. The Major is one
of the jolliest fellows I ever knew. This regiment has seen no fighting yet, and we have been
aroused by no midnight attacks except the diar-
rhea. I don't think myself we shall see any till
spring, as we shall have to go into winter quarters, I expect, about New Year's. Then I should
like you to give me a visit and I'll try to make
it pleasant for you as long as you wish to stay.
* * * * I saw Rem. Taylor, L. C., in Washington about a month ago. I hear very favorably of your business prospects, and with pleasure advise you to "go in boots." Send me a
Standard occasionally.

A letter of November 30th, 1862, to his brother
Stephen from Centreville, Virginia, describes

how he fares with his new command. * * *
"We have been here at Centreville about two
weeks and have our quarters fixed very comfortably.   Colonel and myself have one walled tent
between us; as good on the whole as I had it
last winter, though really we are not yet in winter quarters.   We have plenty of eatables, and
on the whole have nothing to complain of.   I
have had bad luck with my horse, though.   He
has been having hoof-rot, but is getting nearly
well now.   My health is capital, and I weigh one
hundred and sixty-nine pounds.   A perfect monster!   There is no immediate prospect of a fight
just here, and in fact the whole game seems to
be blocked for some reason."

PERSONAL INCIDENTS.

FROM Acquia Creek, Virginia, he writes
to his brother under date of December
30th, 1862, some interesting personal incidents :
* * * "We are still in our old camp here
and nothing remarkable has occurred. I was
sent off with a detachment of two hundred men
last Saturday night to Dumfries to reinforce
Colonel Kennedy there. The night was so dark
I could sometimes hardly see my horse's head,
and in the morning entered Dumfries, but about
an hour too late to find the rebels. After staying there one night we came home again, having
met with no casualties. One good joke: in the
morning we stopped to eat breakfast near a
farm house. The inmates of the house supposed
we were Southerners and fed our horses and us
with great liberality, and when we left expressed

a hope that we'd catch some of the deuced Yankees soon.   They also said that some more of
of 'our folks' (the rebels) had been there about
an hour before.   We carried out the joke, and I
don't know as they've yet found out their mistake, but I think it's highly probable that they
have.

"I understand that my friend Bacon, adjutant
of the Twenty-sixth, has died from wounds received at Fredericksburg.   This makes me feel
very sad.   Both Fessendon and Bacon were very
intimate friends and I feel their loss very keenly.
Bacon was only twenty years of age, and had
just recovered from a wound received at Bull
Run.   What a useless slaughter that affair was!

"I couldn't possibly come home for the holi-
days, as the Colonel himself wished to be away,
but could not get leave.   But if I ever see a
chance I'll come, you may be sure.   I suppose
you've had a first rate time, skating, etc.   A
happy New Year to all!"

February 1st, 1863, finds him at Hartward
Church, Virginia.   The next day he receives a
furlough and visits Washington and his home in
New Jersey.   Afterward, his furlough is extended
to the 21st, and February 24th he is back to his
regiment at Stafford Court House, Virginia.

March 7th, 1863, still at Stafford Court House,

he writes to Stephen : "Our fine weather has left us and mud is again upon us. One month more will end it, though, I suppose. We have had some days that really seemed like spring, and I heard some bluebirds singing in the sunshine. We are in the pine timber now and the smell of the smoke as the March wind blows it in my face reminds me forcibly of burning brush for a new watermelon patch.

"No, you needn't try to tell me anything about mud. I've seen the roads so that it's almost impossible to get along on horseback. I haven't seen Mr. Pearse yet; nor Tom; nor the Twenty-ninth. You see, I'm unfortunately among these Dutchmen. Tell mother my red flannel shirts are much coveted. They are the warmest things I ever wore."

VISIT TO THE TWENTY-NINTH.

MARCH 15th, from the same place, he addresses Stephen, giving an account of his
interesting visit to the Twenty-ninth New Jersey: * * * * "I took a trip over to the
left of the army last week—a ride and a rough
one of about fifteen miles. I called for Tom,
but he was off on leave of absence, so I went
to the Twenty-ninth New Jersey, where I saw
many acquaintances. Rem was sick : Davison,
I thought, was a pretty fine fellow. I guess
they'll all be glad enough when their time is
out, from what I could observe. Every one
seems to have grown fat in the service. They
are very comfortably fixed. I then went to the
Twenty-sixth New York, now reduced to about
two hundred and fifty men, but it was quite sad
to miss the old faces in so many instances. I

had a great time recalling old times, etc., and then a tedious trip home. My horse essays to jump a wide ditch. The mud is slippery where he lands, he slips back into it, and I go over his head, and we're both disgusted with each other. When I got back to camp I found the Colonel had gone off on a leave of absence so I'm in command again for ten days."

March 22d, 1863, writing his brother from Stafford Court House, Virginia, referring to an application made to him through his brother by an acquaintance for an appointment, he states : " For every vacancy that occurs here there are a dozen waiting to step in, and there is always the deuce of a mess whenever it is done. I should feel just so if the Colonel should resign and some other Lieutenant-Colonel should be put over me. What company is he in ? The Ninth is now nowhere near us, but when I once see it again, I'll take occasion to speak a good word for him with his officers. You see, Stevey, that is the best I can do for him without doing injustice to those with whom I am constantly associated. Are you acquainted with Captain Hendrickson of the Ninth ? He lay wounded at Fredericksburg in the same bed with my friend Bacon when he died."

The following extract from a letter written by

a prominent and influential citizen in Madison
County under date of February 23d, 1863, to
Lieutenant-Colonel Arrowsmith, voiced the gen-
eral sentiment of the district from which the
One Hundred and Fifty-seventh was recruited :

" Friend Arrowsmith, you stand well with
your regiment. Every man I have seen speaks
of you in the highest terms. They think you
have some regard for them—that you can sympathize with them, and they not only like you
but they love you. I hope you will cultivate that
feeling and I hope the time is not distant when
for some good reason Lieutenant-Colonel Arrowsmith will be the Colonel of the One Hundred
and Fifty-seventh and that the One Hundred
and Fifty-seventh will then number full one
thousand effective men. I do not wish anything
bad of any other person in order to give you
that place, but if necessary in order for you to
get it, I hope others will be promoted or detailed
to some other duty equally congenial with their
feelings. Your Hamilton friends manifest at
least as much interest in your success as in any
who have gone from Hamilton. Yes, throughout Madison County there is entire satisfaction
in regard to Lieutenant-Colonel Arrowsmith
and there has always been a strong feeling that
he be made Colonel."

March 29th, still at Stafford Court House,
Virginia, with his regiment. Sunday, April 19th,
a letter from camp, One Hundred and Fifty-
seventh New York State Volunteers, closes with
the remark, "I must go to meeting. We have
a first-rate chaplain now."

April 26th, 1863, from Stafford Court House,
Virginia, he again writes his brother *   *   *
"I'm writing in quite a hurry, as we are ordered
to move to-morrow morning early and we have
been here so long that we have accumulated a
great deal of luggage to be taken care of. You
never know, you are aware, how many things
we have till we come to move. I don't know
which way we are going, but I suppose to open
some manœuvre, though in what direction I
know not, so don't expect letters so regularly
after this."

CHANCELLORSVILLE.

THE move referred to and which he supposed was only a manœuvre, was the beginning of the important movement under Hooker towards Chancellorsville. The next day, April 27th, the Eleventh Corps, to which belonged the One Hundred and Fifty-seventh Regiment, under General Howard, moved up the left bank of the Rappahannock to Kelly's ford, where it crossed without opposition. Thence it moved toward Chancellorsville, in light marching order, encumbered with little artillery or baggage, the ammunition being carried by mules, and before the night of the thirtieth they had reached Chancellorsville. May 1st, Hooker's defensive line of battle was formed in shape of the letter C, fronting south. Howard's Corps was on the right and was not only weakly posted but was

considered a weak corps, probably on account
of the raw material that composed it; but as
the enemy were wholly on the Federal left, its
position was unwisely thought to be safe. A
cavalry reconnoissance of the enemy disclosed
the exposed situation of Howard's Corps and
Lee resolved to attack it. Jackson moved at
daybreak of May 2d; by three o'clock in the
afternoon he had moved by forest roads around
the Union army, a circuit of fifteen miles, to a
point within six miles from where he started
and two miles to the west of Howard's position.
Scouts creeping through the woods discovered
the Union intrenchments unguarded. There
was no suspicion of an enemy. The arms were
stacked, the men preparing their dinner. At
five o'clock herds of deer, scared from their
bushy retreats, came rushing over the lines. In
a few minutes Jackson burst upon them through
the woods. The regiments upon whom the
shock first fell scattered without firing a shot,
and the corps broke in disorder and fled. The
pursuit was checked in one quarter by General
Pleasanton with cavalry and artillery; and in
another by General Hooker, who, after vainly
trying to check the fugitives, some of whom
were shot down by his staff, caused Berry's Division to pass straight through the flying crowd
and pour into the woods a fire of artillery which

brought the pursuers to a stand. It was here that Jackson lost his life by the fire of his own men.

On Sunday morning, May 3d, Howard's Corps was on the extreme left of Hooker's line, where no attack was looked for, and it took no further part in the action. On Tuesday night, the Union army recrosses the Rappahannock. Of the five thousand Union soldiers missing in that action, two thousand were from Howard's Corps.

The rout of the Eleventh Corps was owing to an overweening confidence in the safety of its position, on the extreme right of the Union army, while the enemy, being wholly on the Federal left, the possibility of an attack was deemed too remote to be entertained, and in consequence no pickets were posted. This was an inexcusable neglect, especially in view of the fact that at one time during the day, Jackson's long column at one point where his line of march led him over a high hill, was seen by the Federal outposts. It was moving southward as though in full retreat towards Richmond. Still the movement might be meant for an attack upon Howard's position, and he was directed to be upon the alert, and also to throw out pickets on his front—a precaution the neglect of which is unexplained.

Notwithstanding the surprise of the attack

and the great confusion of the flight, the One
Hundred and Fifty-seventh Regiment, though
in action for the first time, acquitted itself with
credit. Its excellent discipline enabled it to
form very quickly, and it stood its ground until
ordered to retreat, when it retreated in good
order, occasionally halting to check the pursuit
of the enemy by a well-directed volley. Night
was coming on, and seeing that they were pursued by only a small detachment, they halted
and charged on the enemy, taking some prisoners. Then it was dark, and they were alone in
a great forest. Selecting a road that led towards
the firing of the battle, bearing their wounded
with them, they finally brought up at Hooker's
headquarters, where they found General Schimmelfenning rallying the Germans. Here they
were publicly thanked by the commanding Generals.

Colonel Arrowsmith, from the beginning to
the end, was at his post of duty, and by his
coolness and intrepidity, inspired his regiment
with the valor of veterans. It was reported as
the verdict of his officers and men, that by his
superior tact and gallant dash, he saved his
regiment from annihilation. Its loss was one
hundred and seven men. In the report of the
action it was highly complimented by the General in command for its good conduct.

Just ten days after leaving Stafford Court House the One Hundred and Fifty-seventh is back there again in its old camp. It has seen stirring times during its short absence, and the first opportunity is now afforded for the Lieutenant-Colonel to write home announcing his safety and the result of "the raid across the river." It is as follows:

> STAFFORD COURT HOUSE, VA., {
> May 7th, 1863. }

Dear Stevey:

All safe and sound yet. I take the pains to tell you of it, for so many rumors are afloat about our corps. We were in the raid across the river, and our corps was badly whipped by being surprised by a sudden attack on our rear while we were carelessly at supper. I'll tell you more when I'm not so sleepy, for there is a great deal to tell. Your brother,   GEORGE.

In accordance with his promise in the last letter to tell more, he writes his brother on May 11th from the same camp, which is not only a valuable contribution to the history of the part taken by the One Hundred and Fifty-seventh in the battle of Chancellorsville, but a full and complete vindication of its honor, courage and soldierly discipline under the most trying circumstances.

HONOR FOR THE 157TH.

" I SUPPOSE you have been informed through the public press of our movements in the crossing of the Rappahannock—of how 'the Eleventh Corps disgraced itself' and no longer 'fights mit Sigel' but 'runs mit Howard.' This in short was owing to three causes—First, miserable generalship; second, miserable fighting; third, having no newspaper reporters.

"We left this camp on Monday and marched to Kelly's ford, built a bridge in the night, drove away the enemy's pickets and crossed over. In the morning, marched towards the Rapidan, skirmishing with the enemy's cavalry. Surprised about one hundred rebels building a bridge at the Rapidan and captured them. Our footmen crossed in the night on the timbers,

our horsemen fording the river and getting
pretty wet. A terrible rain in the night. Thence
to Chancellorsville where we begin to find the
enemy in the woods. We occupy the extreme
right in a wooded country. Friday afternoon
and evening we have some outpost fighting.
Saturday our brigadier is very particular with
his pickets and *reconnoitres* continually, skirmishing all the day long. But there is one place in
our rear, in another division, where there are no
pickets and messengers are sent to report it to
General Howard. He says we do not need any
there, that the attack will be in front. The skirmishing continues all day and attracts but little
attention. About five o'clock we are carelessly
eating supper. The division that had no pickets
was suddenly attacked—Devins's Division—completely bewildered as the rebels came from the
woods right upon their rear. Then they broke.
Their battery, pointed exactly in the wrong
direction, was captured. The artillery horses,
cut loose, ran frantic through the rear line, in-
creasing the confusion. Then some of our German regiments *did* break shamefully at finding
the rebels in their rear and their own officers
killed. We changed front then and resisted the
advance. The Germans fell back and left us
alone. The General who was yet with us then
ordered us to fall back firing, as the enemy had

then got on both our flanks. Then back we
went, occasionally facing about and giving a
volley. As we retreated we got into a woods
The General left us for another part of the field
and no other regiment was around us. Night
was now coming on. General Slocum now engaged the enemy so that only a small detachment pursued us through the forest. As soon
as we found this out, we halted and charged on
them, driving them back and taking four prisoners. Then we were left alone and the question
was which way to go. It was dark, we had no
compass and it was a matter of some importance
which army we should come upon. The battle
was still going on and we took a wood road and
went towards the firing, taking our wounded
with us. We had the good luck to come near
Hooker's headquarters, where we found Schimmelfenning rallying the Germans. Here the
generals publicly thanked the field officers and
the regiment generally. So this is the second
time I have had the luck to gain credit in a defeat, but there isn't much consolation in it. Our
regiment is much honored in the corps, but
we're all in disgrace together and I wish we
were clear of the Dutch. The Dutch are blam-
ing Howard for his negligence and he blames
the Germans for breaking. They are both right.
We are out of the quarrel and they both praise

us. To make matters worse the newspaper reporters in the employ of Hooker and Howard
have laid the *whole* blame on the troops, but that
will come all right in time. The upshot of the
whole was, the Eleventh Corps was shamefully
beaten ; the One Hundred and Fifty-seventh
has derived credit from it though with the loss
of one hundred and seven men. I was not
scratched. Colonel Brown was very slightly in-
jured on the arm by a spent shot. On Sunday,
Monday and Tuesday the battles were successes,
but the original plan was foiled and the whole
army safely re-crossed the river, and we were
out from under fire again. The slaughter among
the rebels I've no doubt was terrible. Howard
is much blamed for his negligence. Instead of
our flank being reinforced, one brigade was sent
during the day to strengthen Sickles."

Captain George L. Warner, of Cortland, New
York, is one of the few surviving officers of the
One Hundred and Fifty-seventh Regiment. He
is now secretary of the regimental association,
and he has kindly favored me with a letter con-
taining some of his recollections of Lieutenant-
Colonel Arrowsmith and the One Hundred and
Fifty-seventh at Chancellorsville, from which I
make a few extracts that may be of interest.
*   *   *   *   "I well remember the battle of

Chancellorsville. I was First Lieutenant in a company at that time, and saw Arrowsmith in the hottest part of the fight. I can answer for his coolness under fire, inspiring confidence among the officers and men by his example. On the first day at Chancellorsville we were in column *en masse*, facing south, when we were struck by Jackson on the right flank. We immediately fell in. Our right rested on a thick grove, and we started to face the advancing enemy. The underbrush was so thick that we had to move by the flank, in a wood road, and the brush on either side was so thick that it was impossible to get away from the lane, when we were met first with one or two wounded horses, that jumped right into the ranks. You can imagine the result. This was followed up by minie bullets. We retreated back to the clearing, where we had been all day, and made a stand, firing several volleys into the advancing column, by which we held them till the main body came up; they having the woods and we the open field and within rifle range, the advantage was all on their side. We again fell back, and when they came out of the woods, we made another stand and gave the enemy some punishment. We here lost several men. Then we fell back to the Chancellorsville house, and the lines were formed. Arrowsmith was always at his post of duty. I do not think that there was ever the slightest misunderstanding between the Colonel, Lieutenant-Colonel and Major. They always pulled together, and throughout the One Hundred and Fifty-seventh there were never any dissensions. I attribute this in a great measure to the influence of Lieutenant-Colonel Arrowsmith. If Major Carmichael were living he could tell you a great deal more than I can, for he was with him most of the time, but he died two years ago; also Captain Coffin, who died several years since; and there are but two of the original captains living, Frank Place of Cortland, and L. F. Briggs of Eaton, Madison County, New York, who was at Gettysburg, and left on the field badly wounded. I was promoted to the captaincy in the latter part of 1864. As lieutenant I did not have much social intercourse with the field officers, but I was always received by Colonel Arrowsmith with the same cordiality as though I had been an officer of equal rank, which was one of his peculiar characteristics. It was equally so with the enlisted men, and I never heard an unkind word from any member of the One Hundred and Fifty-seventh, officer or private, concerning Colonel Arrowsmith."

May 17th, from camp near Brooks Station, Virginia, the Lieutenant-Colonel writes that they have moved their camp for sanitary reasons, about a mile from their former camp, in a splendid place. "What a beautiful Sunday!" he writes. "The birds singing and the sun shining." He speaks of a visit to his brother Tom, who had returned from a raid, and who had given him one of his horses to keep for him, which he was glad to do. During the last week, he states, he has been acting as president of a Court Martial. Referring to the rout of the Eleventh Corps, he says: "Nothing new. Time and truth are working a little in favor of the Eleventh Corps, but truth will never help some regiments in it. We have the assurance from the Generals that ours will be most favorably mentioned in the reports, so on that we rest."

May 24th, writing from the same place, he says: "We have a splendid camp, adorned with evergreens like an ice cream garden. The Colonel is off on a ten-days' leave, and I am in command. The indications are that we shall do nothing for some time, at least. The pickets are reduced and we're taking our ease. Schurtz has his wife here."

Another letter from the same place, under date of May 31st, 1863, his mind recurs to the defeat of the Eleventh Corps. * * * "You will perceive that there is now a more rational opinion afloat with regard to the Eleventh Corps.

I must confess the corps didn't do to suit me,
for it was the duty of the corps to remain there
and die under the circumstances. Still, out of
justice to the many that fell there, the eighty-
three from my own regiment, a wholesale con-
demnation is hardly fair. We had the misfor-
tune to occupy the critical position under a
corps general, who never before commanded a
corps, and a commander-in-chief who never before commanded an army. I think some other
corps might have stood there fifteen minutes
longer, only that, for Jackson's whole army was
upon us. The Germans also would not have
acted so under Sigel."   *   *   *

THE results of the battles of Fredericksburg and Chancellorsville inspired the most sanguine hopes at Richmond, and it was resolved to renew the invasion of the North upon a scale that would enable the South to conquer peace and dictate its terms. Early in June Lee's army began its northward march, moving down the valley of the Shenandoah westward of the Blue Ridge Mountains. The Union army followed in a parallel direction on the opposite side of the Blue Ridge.

On the twenty-first of June the One Hundred and Fifty-seventh was at Goose Creek, Virginia, about six miles south of Leesburg. Here our Lieutenant-Colonel writes to his brother: "We are in a bivouac along the stream about six miles from Leesburg, but we do not expect to stay here long. I hear some fighting now in the direction of Aldie. Pleasanton's cavalry, I guess. I went on a scout over in Maryland last week, with one cavalryman, swimming our horses over the Potomac. We had a first-rate time, but were arrested by our own cavalry as spies over the river. We got back all safe yesterday afternoon. I saw the Twenty-ninth just before they started. I think they had better come back again. All well, and right."

On the twenty-fourth and twenty-fifth of June the confederate army crossed the Potomac, near the battle field of Antietam, and pressed on towards Chambersburg in Pennsylvania. On the twenty-sixth Hooker crossed the Potomac at Edwards Ferry, and moved towards Frederick City. The next day Hooker resigned the command of the army, and General Meade was appointed in his stead. Howard retained the command of the Eleventh Corps. A portion of Lee's army had reached Carlisle, Pa., and was preparing to move on Harrisburg, but the news that Meade had crossed the Potomac, and was advancing northward, compelled him to change his plans and move towards Gettysburg. On the twenty-eighth of June a portion of Hooker's corps, including the One Hundred and Fifty-seventh New York, had reached Mid-

dletown, Maryland. From this point the Lieutenant-Colonel writes his last letter home. It
is addressed as usual to "Dear Stevey" and
was written on Sunday, just three days before
the battle, but it was not received by his brother
until after the melancholy news of his death.
In it he writes:

"Well, we are in Maryland. In as fine a country as I ever saw in my life—like Pleasant Valley—quite refreshing—abundance of everything
—nearly all Union people—stars and stripes
hanging out all over—hotels open—no robbing
on the one side, and no bushwhacking on the
other; quite a pleasant change for the army, but
quite bad for the country generally. Middletown is a nice place, about like Middletown
Point, and the people are nearly all Unionists,
so it is very pleasant. I have been a little unwell for a day or two, and have been staying at
a private house, but am all right again now, and
expect to return to camp to-morrow. Write
soon."

How rejoiced must have been these worn and
travel-stained troops, after two years of campaigning upon the battle-scarred fields of Virginia, hot and smoking amid the desolations of
war, to find themselves surrounded by green
pastures and fields of bending grain. Loud

and long must have been their cheers and their songs, as the Union-loving citizens of Maryland greeted them with the emblems of loyalty from every housetop and window, and spread before them the richest bounties of their generous hospitality. As the Lieutenant-Colonel expresses it, there was no bushwhacking, no robbing, now, for the boys in blue, for the first time, were campaigning among their friends.

THE BATTLE OF GETTYSBURG.

ON the night of June 30th, General Howard's Corps was supporting the First, and lay at Emmetsburg, ten miles south of Gettysburg, with orders to march up and keep within supporting distance of the First Corps. On the morning of the first of July it left Emmetsburg and marched to Gettysburg. On the way they caught the sound of artillery firing. It was the First Corps engaging the enemy. Lieutenant-Colonel Arrowsmith had not fully recovered from his illness at Middletown, but he felt able to ride his horse. Dr. II. C. Hendrick, the regimental surgeon, rode by his side. Hearing heavy cannonading Arrowsmith remarked, "There will be warm work to-day, Doctor." The doctor replied : "You must not go into the fight, Colonel; you are not strong enough." As

they proceeded, Colonel Arrowsmith talked
freely and spoke of the trepidation usually experienced upon going into battle the first time.
"I have gotten over all that," said he. "I have
come to feel that the bullet is not moulded
which is to kill me." *

The regiment reached Gettysburg about noon,
much fatigued with a rapid march on a mid-
summer day. An order is given to double-quick
march. They take to the sidewalks. Captain
Dilger's First Ohio Battery, which was behind,
sweeps by them on a swift gallop, its cannoniers
bouncing high in their seats as the wheels re-
volve rapidly over obstructions in the roadway.
The men of the One Hundred and Fifty-seventh
swing their hats in the air with loud cheers for
the First Ohio Battery. They know each other,
for they were together at Chancellorsville.
They pass through the town to a point a few
hundred yards north of it, where three roads
come together. The Mummasburg road branch-
ing to the northwest; the Carlisle road to the
north, and the Harrisburg road to the northeast.
In the double triangle thus formed the Eleventh
Corps took its position facing northward, the
One Hundred and Fifty-seventh Regiment being
posted in a field on the right of the First Corps,

---

* Appendix, Note E.

with the Mummasburg road on its left and the Carlisle road on its right, while the First Ohio Battery was immediately in its front. The shell from the guns of the enemy flew over the battery and fell in the regiment, doing much injury, and on account of the horses becoming restless, Colonel Brown and Lieutenant-Colonel Arrowsmith dismounted and sent their animals to the rear. The first shot from the Ohio Battery flew over the confederate battery. At this the rebels were jubilant and yelled in derision. Captain Dilger now sighted the gun himself and fired it. The shot dismounted a rebel gun and killed the horses. Captain Dilger tried it a second time, sighting and firing the gun. No effect being visible with the naked eye, Colonel Brown, who was near, asked "What effect, Captain Dilger?" Captain, after looking through his glass, replied, "I have spiked a gun for them, plugging it at the muzzle." In the first movement of the regiment on the left of the field two hundred rebels came in and surrendered themselves as prisoners. Once, under fire, while executing a manœuvre, the regiment fell into confusion, from which there seemed to be difficulty in extricating it. Then was heard the stentorian voice of the Lieutenant-Colonel conveying the right order at the right moment, which immediately relieved the embarrassment. A sur-

vivor of the regiment relating the incident says,
" Oh, how glad we were to hear that voice, for
then we knew that our beloved Lieutenant-
Colonel, who had been ill, was with us." *

During the forenoon, the First Corps had
more than held its own, driving the enemy and
capturing many prisoners. About ten o'clock
rebel reinforcements began to arrive. Rodes
and Early had come up by a rapid march.
Rodes's Division entered the fight about noon.
The First Corps, now greatly outnumbered and
hard pressed, was about giving way on its right.
It was at this juncture the Eleventh Corps arrived. By their support the tide of battle was
stayed. It was now two o'clock. Early's Division then advanced, forming in front of Schurtz's
Division.

It was impossible for the First Corps and two
divisions of the Eleventh Corps, comprising not
more than eighteen thousand men, to stand long
before forty thousand of Heath, Pender, Rodes
and Early. , General Howard wisely recognizing
this fact, before any order of retreat had been
given, directed the withdrawal of the heavy artillery to Cemetery Hill, and so disposed of
Steinwehr's Division that it could support our
retiring men.

---

* Appendix, Note F.

DEATH OF ARROWSMITH.

EARLY'S Division now entered the fight.
The Federal line was sorely pressed. It
took the form of a crescent, its extreme points
being drawn in towards the town, while the centre, which was the position of the One Hundred
and Fifty-seventh, was in danger of being cut
off altogether by the confederate attack upon
both flanks. The enemy was seen advancing
toward the town by the right flank, driving the
Second Brigade. General Schimmelfenning ordered the regiment to move over to the right to
check their advance. It proceeded to execute
the order and moved up to within fifty yards of
the enemy. The attack was made. Colonel
Arrowsmith was on the right of the line. His
voice was heard above the din of the battle, encouraging the men and directing their fire. The

regiment was in an exposed place and suffering
fearful slaughter by the enemy's fire upon both
flanks. After fighting a short time Colonel Arrowsmith fell, struck by a rifle ball in the fore-
head. A general retreat had been ordered, but
the aide bearing the order had his horse shot
under him and it did not reach the brigade
promptly. It came at last and the regiment retreated. The following letter from Colonel
Brown, written twenty-four days after the battle,
but hitherto unpublished, was intended to give
to the public the particulars concerning Colonel
Arrowsmith's death:

WASHINGTON, D. C., July 27th, 1863.
Mr. Editor:

As several incorrect reports have been made
with reference to the death of Lieutenant-
Colonel Arrowsmith, I thought it would be gratifying to his friends to know all the particulars
just as they are. The morning of the day on
which the battle occurred, the regiment marched
from Emmetsburg, a distance of ten miles,
reaching Gettysburg very much worried. The
greatly superior numbers against which the First
Corps were contending made it necessary for
the Eleventh to be thrown promptly forward.
Without stopping for rest we were moved
through the town upon the double quick and

placed in position behind Dilger's Battery, which was soon engaged by three batteries of the enemy. While lying there the numerous shot and shell thrown among us rendered our horses so unmanageable we both dismounted and sent them to the rear. After the rebel batteries had been silenced the whole brigade was thrown forward. Soon after reaching the position assigned us I was ordered by General Schimmelfenning to move over some distance to the right and attack the enemy, who were then driving the Second Brigade of our Division. This order I proceeded at once to execute. In order to get my regiment into position to do effective service, I found it necessary to move up to within fifty yards of the enemy, who by the time I reached my position had placed a whole brigade in line to resist my attack. The attack was made, Colonel Arrowsmith occupying his proper position on the right, encouraging his men and faithfully and gallantly doing his whole duty, while I gave my attention to the centre and left. We had been fighting but a short time, when, upon looking to the right, I discovered that the Lieutenant-Colonel was missing. I moved at once to the right and found him lying upon his back, badly wounded in the head, breathing slowly and heavily, and evidently insensible. As my presence along the line was

more necessary that he had fallen, I could stop
but a moment, and returned to my position.
The men were falling rapidly and the enemy's
line was taking the form of a semi-circle, evidently with the design of surrounding us, at the
same time concentrating the fire of their whole
brigade upon my rapidly diminishing numbers.
An enfilading fire from a battery upon our left
was also doing fearful execution. I had looked
around several times to see if some support
would not be sent, or an order for retreat.
Neither came. The last time I looked I saw
one of General Schimmelfenning's aides about
half way across the field, taking the saddle off
his horse and running back, and I learned from
some of my wounded men who fell before we
reached our position, that the same aide came
out a short distance and hallooed to me to retreat. I, however, heard no order. Seeing that
we were likely to be all shot down or taken
prisoners, I ordered a retreat. From the wounded left on the field I learned that the Lieutenant-
Colonel died shortly after the retreat. An attempt was made to bring him off, but the prox-
imity of the enemy and the hot firing prevented.
Lieutenant-Colonel Arrowsmith died, as every
true soldier would wish to die, at his post, gallantly fighting for his country. A brave man, a
skillful officer, possessing a keen sense of honor,

generous to a fault, bound to him by a long personal attachment formed and ripened in the
various relations of teachers and pupils, associate teachers and fellow officers, I mourn his
loss as that of a brother, and offer to the family
and friends of the lamented hero my warmest
and tenderest sympathy.

I am, sir, with great respect,

Your obedient servant,

P. P. BROWN, JR.,

Col. 157th N. Y. Vols.

I am indebted to Lieutenant-Colonel Frank
Place of Cortland, New York, for another account of Colonel Arrowsmith's death and of the
part of the One Hundred and Fifty-seventh in
the first day's battle of Gettysburg. Lieutenant-Colonel Place was the senior captain in the
regiment at that time and a warm personal
friend of Colonel Arrowsmith. He writes
* * * "Our corps (Eleventh) came up from
Emmetsburg at about noon, passed through the
town and took position on the right of the First
Corps, my own regiment deploying into the
field east of the Mummasburg road and just opposite the Pennsylvania College. We were soon
moved further east—as far as the Carlisle road,
and there supported the battery belonging to
our brigade. After an hour or so the battery

and my regiment were ordered forward, towards the hill between these two roads, the battery was withdrawn and my regiment continued to advance. Soon it was discovered that the enemy were advancing towards the town by our right flank. We were ordered by the Colonel to 'change front forward on first company,' all the while under fire apparently on both flanks. It was while this movement was being executed or just after that Lieutenant-Colonel Arrowsmith received the fatal shot. He was near the right of the line. I think that he never stirred after he fell. I was within ten feet of him when he fell. I was the Senior Captain in the regiment and was in my place, but having the command of my men, I could render him no assistance. My recollection is that orders to retreat very soon reached us and we left the field.

"My First Lieutenant, J. A. Coffin, was wounded and left upon the field. He recovered after a while and found Colonel Arrowsmith's body, and took from his person his D. K. E. badge. Coffin and I were both captured and spent nine months together in Libby Prison. I was then exchanged and Coffin stayed nearly a year longer. I believe that the Lieutenant-Colonel's badge was sent to his brother.

"The field officers dismounted before going into this fight. Colonel Brown was in command. Colonel Arrowsmith was in his place and in the line of duty when killed. No braver or cooler man ever breathed. ' Why were we in such an exposed position ?' We were ordered to advance, and receiving no order to retire, we kept advancing. The General sent an aide with orders for us to retreat, but his horse was shot under him and he was delayed in giving us the order. In the meantime Colonel Brown, seeing the advance of rebel troops along the Carlisle road, ordered us to change front. Then receiving orders to retreat, we did retreat.

"Now I have given you briefly an account of Colonel Arrowsmith's death, etc. A captain in command of his company has all he can do in that line. He has no time to take in the whole plan of battle, and hence I may not be able to give all that transpired, but I have done this as faithfully as I can. There are many things I might say with regard to Colonel Arrowsmith's character, if my pen were adequate. Let me say that no officer of the One Hundred and Fifty-seventh Regiment enjoyed the confidence and respect of the men in a greater degree than did Lieutenant Colonel George Arrowsmith."

The field officers of the One Hundred and Fifty-seventh Regiment on the morning of the first of July, 1863, Colonel Place states, were as

follows: P. P. Brown, Jr., colonel, commanding; George Arrowsmith, lieutenant - colonel;
J. C. Carmichael, major on the staff of General
Schurtz. After the death of Colonel Arrowsmith, Major Carmichael was promoted to the
vacant Lieutenant-Colonelcy and Captain Place
was commissioned major early in 1865. Colonel
Brown resigned to take a command in General
Hancock's veteran corps. Lieutenant-Colonel
Carmichael was commissioned colonel and Major
Place was commissioned lieutenant-colonel of
the One Hundred and Fifty-seventh Regiment,
but neither of the last two were ever mustered
into the rank to which they had been commissioned.

"When the regiment reached town," says
Colonel Place, "we found the east portion of
the village already in possession of the confederate troops and pressing close on the west.
Many were captured in the town. General
Schimmelfenning, commanding the brigade,
concealed himself in a woodpile and remained
there until the evacuation on the morning of the
fourth day."

That portion of the First and Eleventh Corps
which escaped, made a stand on Cemetery Hill.
Meade's army got into position that night from
Culp's Hill to Round Top, and the next day the

battle began on more equal terms, with the result that the world knows.

The One Hundred and Fifty-seventh Regiment was almost annihilated. Its loss was as follows : Killed—four officers and twenty-three enlisted men ; wounded—eight officers and one hundred and fifty-eight enlisted men ; captured —six officers and one hundred and eight enlisted men. Aggregate of killed, wounded and captured, three hundred and seven, out of about three hundred and fifty with which it entered the battle.*

Lieutenant Coffin, the wounded officer who went to the assistance of Colonel Arrowsmith after he fell, besides the Delta Kappa Epsilon badge, took possession of some other articles of property found upon his person and which he knew would be cherished as relics of the dying hero. Among these were his revolver, his shoulder straps, and a little book stained with his blood entitled, "A Memorial of Adjutant Bacon," which on a fly-leaf bore the following inscription: "To my esteemed friend, Lieutenant-Colonel George Arrowsmith, a beloved associate and companion in arms of my brave and loyal son, this memorial of him is presented by the author, June, 1863." These he sacredly guarded

---

* Appendix, Note G.

during his captivity, until opportunity was found
to forward them to the parents of the deceased.
One of the shoulder straps had been cut by a
rifle ball in the battle, causing a slight abrasion
of the shoulder, evidencing the terrific character
of the enemy's fire; but before Lieutenant
Coffin had secured these relics, a wounded private had taken the ring from Colonel Arrowsmith's finger, and his purse from his pocket,
containing about one hundred and sixty dollars.
As the field was in the possession of the enemy,
he saw no harm in taking this property from the
dead officer, as they were sure to be taken and
confiscated by the enemy.   The harm lay in
the criminal appropriation of the property thus
secured.   The wounded culprit found his way
to a Newark military hospital.   He gave the
empty purse to a fellow soldier, with the remark,
"If you knew who it belonged to you would
prize it."   He also exhibited the ring upon his
finger, remarking that "he thought a great deal
of it, for it belonged to the best man in his regiment."   These facts having been reported, earnest efforts were made to obtain the property.
Finally, by the effective exertions of Marcus L.
Ward, afterwards Governor of New Jersey, a
confession was extorted from the criminal.   The
money he had spent, with the exception of about
seventy-five dollars, which was restored, and the

ring, though it had been given away, was recovered.

The sword presented to Lieutenant-Colonel
Arrowsmith by his men when he was Captain of
Company D, Twenty-sixth New York Regiment,
has a history. At his promotion, having no further personal use for it, he loaned it to his friend,
Byron S. Fitch, Second Lieutenant Company
C, One Hundred and Fifty-seventh New York
Volunteers, who carried it in the battle of
Gettysburg. When he saw the certainty of his
capture by the enemy, he buried it in an ash-heap
in the street at Gettysburg. He was captured,
but succeeded in escaping before the evacuation
of the town. After the retreat of the confederates, he returned to the ash-heap and recovered
the hidden treasure.

Upon receiving the sorrowful news of his
brother's decease, Dr. Joseph E. Arrowsmith
hastened to the scene of the late conflict. Arriving at Baltimore on the Fourth of July, he was
subjected to much delay and difficulty in reaching Gettysburg, as all lines of travel were sub-
ordinated to military authority, and transporta-
tion to civilians was denied. He did not reach
the battle ground until late the following week,
whence he proceeded to the hospital of the
Eleventh Army Corps, two miles south of Gettysburg, to obtain information respecting the place

of burial of his brother. Of this visit the New York *Herald* related the following incident in an obituary notice of the deceased :

" A touching incident which occurred well illustrates the estimation in which the deceased was held by officers and men. It was in the hospital of the Eleventh Army Corps, about two miles south of Gettysburg. The surgeons were working hard with the wounded, many of whom had been four or five days awaiting surgical aid. Of course they were anxiously looking for relief. A private of the One Hundred and Fifty-seventh New York, after so long waiting, had now reached his turn, and was just going to be laid on the operator's table. Hearing that friends of his late Lieutenant-Colonel were inquiring where the body fell and was buried, he at once volunteered to go and show them. Of course the offer of the noble hearted man was not accepted. Instantly Captain Adams, who had just been taken off the operator's table, where he had had a ball extracted, which, after a circuitous route, had lodged under the shoulder blade, tendered his services to point out the place. And in this condition he went."

The body was exhumed, and decomposition had progressed to an extent that rendered neces-

sary a metallic coffin. The supply of these in
Gettysburg and Baltimore was unequal to the
demand. The doctor was compelled to go back
to New York for the purpose of procuring one :
and then returning, he caused the remains to be
forwarded to Middletown, New Jersey.

FUNERAL OBSEQUIES.

THE funeral obsequies were held in the Baptist Church of Middletown, on Sunday, July 26th, 1863, at half-past three o'clock. The weather was propitious, and the assembled throng was so great that but a small part could find accommodation within the church edifice. The Brigade Board of Monmouth and Ocean Counties was present in full uniform without side arms. An impressive sermon was delivered by the Rev. David B. Stout,* and an obituary notice, rendering tribute to the exalted character of the deceased, was read by the Rev. Dr. Samuel Lockwood. After the service the remains were interred at Fair View cemetery in Middletown township. Quite extended obituary

* Appendix, Note A.

notices of a highly eulogistic character appeared in the newspapers of Madison, Cortland and Chemung Counties of New York, and Monmouth County, New Jersey ; also in the daily papers of New York City, Washington and Philadelphia. Resolutions of condolence and respect were adopted by the Brigade Board of Monmouth and Ocean Counties,* and by the Class of '59 of Madison University,† of which the deceased was a member, at the Commencement following his death. In commemoration of his virtues and noble deeds a monument of Quincy granite was erected over his remains. It bears the following inscription :

LT. COL. GEORGE ARROWSMITH,

ONE HUNDRED AND FIFTY-SEVENTH NEW YORK VOLUNTEERS.

He bore a distinguished part in several severe engage-ments, and fell at Gettysburg gallantly leading his Regi-ment, July 1st, 1863, aged 24 years, 2 months, 13 days.

Erected by his numerous friends in token of his personal worth, patriotic devotion, and distinguished bravery.

The devoted regiment and his college asso-ciates made generous contributions towards its expense as a tribute of their love.

---

* Appendix, Note H. † Note I.

TRIBUTE FROM COLONEL PLACE.

" PUNCTILIOUS in all that appertained to military discipline and etiquette in the line of duty, he could meet the humblest private soldier at other times on terms of equality. He was in no sense a-martinet. He was modest without being weak, conscious of his personality and power, without being arrogant and obtrusive.

"I soon learned that there were ties which bound me to him other than those of a common humanity or loyalty to the flag we had both sworn to defend ; that we were members of the same college fraternity. To us twain fraternity, charity and loyalty had a twofold meaning.

"He possessed all the qualities of a thorough disciplinarian, and held the line officers to a strict accountability for their conduct in the

presence of their men in all the minor duties of
camp, bivouac, or drill. He never publicly re-
proved an officer, but sought the retirement of
his tent to administer a rebuke for any un-
soldierly conduct. The peculiar bond between
him and myself above referred to did not in the
least exempt me from receiving deserved re-
proof. He thoroughly believed in the potent
influence of example upon the rank and file set
by those in authority over them. This principle
he exemplified at all times, and in all places. It
is an historical fact that at Chancellorsville our
army was surprised. The enemy made their
attack from the direction not contemplated, and
hence we were in no position to repel.

"The result was a defeat. This was the first
general engagement in which my regiment had
participated. The attack came suddenly and
with overpowering effect, yet I can confidently
assert that it was largely through Colonel Arrowsmith's coolness and self-possession that we retreated from that ill-fated field in so good order
and with so little loss of life. Our next general
engagement was at Gettysburg, Pennsylvania,
July 1st, 1863. Here Colonel Arrowsmith displayed the same courageous qualities that distinguished him at Chancellorsville. He died as
he would have chosen to die if so willed, with
his face towards the foe. Thus he filled the full

measure of devotion to his country, by the sacrifice not only of the hopes and aspirations of the
cultured and refined gentleman, but of life itself."

Colonel Place addressed the Arrowsmith Post
as follows :

*"Comrades of Arrowsmith Post, Department of New
Jersey, Grand Army of the Republic :*

"You acted wisely when you decided upon
the name of your Post. The name of George
Arrowsmith is enshrined in the hearts of his surviving comrades. No words of mine can add
lustre to his renown. I can only exhort you to
emulate his patriotic devotion to the cause of
your country's welfare and prosperity."

CONCLUSION.

THUS lived and died Lieutenant - Colonel George Arrowsmith at the early age of twenty-four 'years. While full maturity of character had not been attained, yet there was exhibited a sound and vigorous growth, beautiful in its symmetry, and towering in its aspirations. Though falling in the springtime of life, he did not live in vain. The principle for which he grasped his sword was vindicated. The rebellion was crushed and constitutional liberty was preserved. It was he in common with other brave hearts and strong arms who accomplished this great result. He lived long enough to share in the glorious work and to render brilliantly conspicuous the virtues of his noble character.

He gave his *all* to his country, cultivated talents, alluring prospects in civil pursuits, a

young life ; as a patriot he could have done no
more. Of his courage I need not speak. It is
attested by heroic deeds on several battle-fields,
which are at once his monuments and his eu-
logies.

In manhood he was the soul of honor, with an
innate contempt for whatever was mean or in-
triguing. He possessed a high sense of duty
which characterized his whole life, a steady purpose to do what he believed to be right. He
honored his father and mother, and in the sacred
precincts of his own home he was the light and
joy of their hearts.

There was no gulf between him and others of
less favored position. He had no snobbish pride
or silly vanity. Here he was the idol of the
volunteer soldier. He possessed a dignity in
bearing and a gravity in repose, but when approached his genial salutation relieved all un-
certainty. He was proud, but it was the honorable pride born of true nobility of character.
He was ambitious, but it was the laudable ambition to excel in good works and deeds.

In conversation and social intercourse he was
refined and courteous. A coarse or profane expression never fell from his lips. It was a strong
point made in one of the testimonials presented
to Governor Morgan recommending his pro-

motion, that he was an officer who never used profane language.

His knowledge of history and general English literature was extensive. He had a good memory, keen perceptions and a pleasant vein of humor. To these he united gifts of soul that enabled him to bind to his heart all who knew him with bands of steel.

His patriotism was not the enthusiasm of the hour to be chilled by the first reverse or defeat. It was a settled determination, a firm conviction, that underlying the contest was a great moral principle. Scenes of peril, of exposure, of exertion, he encountered without a murmur. Nor did he entertain a thought of terminating his military career before the end of the war. To the advice of a friend that he should limit his term of service, his reply was that "as long as the war lasts, I will serve my country."

His natural qualities were conspicuously manifested in his army life. From the patient and painstaking student he became a thorough instructor and tactician in camp. From a genial companion in society he passed as the type of good fellowship by the camp-fire. His gentle and sympathetic nature endeared him to the victims of pain and suffering. Favored with a strong physical organization, he could endure hardships without exhaustion. Possessed of great moral pride, he was a lion in danger, and his natural impetuosity made him a thunderbolt in battle.

It is idle to speculate upon what he might have been had his life been spared. We accept him with admiration and gratitude for what he was. Enlisting as a mere boy, without rank, he was at once unanimously chosen by his fellow volunteers as the commandant of the company. In one year, for merit, he was promoted to the office of Assistant Adjutant-General upon the staff of General Tower, upon the recommendation of the Division Commander, General Ricketts. Without leaving the army, he was elevated to the field office of Lieutenant-Colonel by the Governor of New York, who was thus prompted by the fame of the soldier, and was only restrained from appointing him Colonel by his generous refusal to accept the position over a friend. On the eve of Gettysburg his comrades urged his higher promotion, with flattering testimonials from persons of distinguished military rank, but here was ended his rising career. It was an honorable death, and his epitaph is briefly written : a sterling soldier, a true patriot, and a brave man.

APPENDIX.

NOTE A.

A sermon by the Rev. David B. Stout on the occasion of the funeral of the late Lieutenant-Colonel George Arrowsmith. Text, II Samuel, chapter xix, verse 2. "And the victory that day was turned into mourning unto all the people."

It is a fact attested by universal experience, that by sympathy a man may receive into his own affectionate feelings a measure of the distress of his friend, and that his friend does find himself relieved in the same proportion as the other has entered into his grief. From the language of the text I would call your attention to the duty of Christian sympathy toward the bereaved.

There is in the heart of man a generous sympathy for man. By sympathy is meant fellow-feeling—the quality of being affected by feelings similar to those of another. By observing the operations of our own minds, we shall discover the existence of this principle, and become convinced that it is a distinct element of human nature.

A smile upon the countenance of a friend excites one
upon our own. The depiction of sorrow and deep dejec-
tion upon the visage of a fellow being, measurably produces to some extent similar feelings in our own hearts.
If we are present on occasions of peculiar joy to our
friends, we, by the sympathy of our nature, partake of
that joy. No one with a full knowledge of the circumstances could have witnessed the countenance of the
venerable patriarch brightening with a beam of joy, as
he listened to the narration of his sons, late from Egypt,
and lifted up his eyes and saw the wagons sent for his
accommodation, and heard him in the exuberance of
paternal joy exclaim, " It is enough, Joseph, my son, is
yet alive, I will go and see him before I die," without
having felt the movings of inward sympathy and a thrill
of sadness. Our grief is also excited by witnessing the
grief of others. Visit the dwelling of a respected acquaintance; enter the apartment where with esteemed
friends and a beloved family you have been accustomed
to spend the social hour. Beside the farthermost wall of
that apartment, fix your eyes upon the concealed form of
one whom conjugal and paternal fidelity the day previous had employed in the active duties of life. Approach,
withdraw the covering which conceals the well-known
features of your friend, still unchanged, and perfect in
their form, save that the eye has gathered dimness, and
closed itself upon the world forever, and the livid hue has
given place to a death-like paleness. With the disclosure
of those familiar features, listen to the sobs of the new
made widow and orphan children. Witness the deep
and irrepressible agony of a bereaved heart, venting itself in a flood of tears, and the sympathies of your
nature will be awakened and you will heave an involun-
tary sigh, and drop a spontaneous tear.

This element of our nature is an endowment of crea-
tive wisdom and goodness; it subserves valuable purposes and aids in the performance of essential duties;
it is adapted to the social nature of man, and is promo-
tive of the social virtues; it awakens in the different
members of the human family a reciprocal interest in
each other's welfare, chastened by pure religion; it "re-
joices with those who rejoice, and weeps with those who
weep;" it fosters kindness, generosity and benevolence,
but is pained to witness suffering in any form, and unhappy as it listens to the tale of war; it is aroused into
vigorous action by unexpected and disastrous events, by
which aggravated suffering is produced, and the lives of
our fellow beings lost. The text expresses its language
on such an occasion. In the fortunes of war David's son
had fallen, and though the circumstances of his rebellion
and his death were such as would seem to destroy the
exercise of sympathy, yet the event has fully proven that
the parental relation rises superior to all others; for as
the men of Judah marched out of the gate of the city of
Mahamin, in companies of hundreds and of thousands,
led by their Commander Joab, David stood by the gate
and said, "Deal gently with the young man, even with
Absalom." And all the people heard when the King gave
all the captains charge concerning Absalom. How strong
is the bond of parental affection! David, by the skill
and valor of his troops, had gained a complete victory;
nothing could be more seasonable or important. It
crushed the wide-spread rebellion and reduced his subjects to allegiance. But behold the King ! All suspense,
sitting between the two gates waiting for intelligence.
Two messengers run to announce the victory. The first
said "all is well." Which was saying the victory is ours !
our foes are subdued ! That was very important. But

another inquiry lying deep down in his anxious spirit,
breaks forth from his lips.   " Is the young man Absalom
safe ?"   This was a question too great for the moral courage of the messenger, and he evades it.

The second messenger has now arrived.   "Tidings,
my Lord, the King, for the Lord hath avenged thee this
day of all them that rose up against thee."   But his heart
is still bursting with anxiety for a reply to his unanswered
question, hence he repeats it.   " Is the young man Absalom safe?"   And Cushi said, "The enemies of my
Lord, the King, and all that rise against thee to do thee
hurt, be as that young man is."   Nothing could have
been more wise or delicate than the manner in which the
truth was insinuated !   But like a sword, it pierced
through David's soul and the King was much moved,
and went up to the chamber over the gate and wept;
and as he went, thus he said, " O my son Absalom ! My
son, my son Absalom ! would God I had died for thee.
O Absalom, my son, my son !"

David stood in a double relation; he was not only a
King, but a father; and though Absalom had been an undutiful child, still he was a child; and for a child to be
cut off, not only in the midst of his days, but in the midst
of his sins, was painful in the extreme.   Excuse or con-
demn David for his conduct on this occasion, the event
is the same; "And the victory that day was turned into
mourning unto all the people."

Secondly—this is true, to a certain extent, of every
national victory.   When two large armies are drawn up
in battle array, with all their improved appliances of death
and slaughter, to use the language of Scripture, " The
land mourns."   Fields are ravaged, fences destroyed,
houses demolished, women and children fly.   Mournful
is the infliction of pain, while thousands are agonizing

together upon the gory field, where they often lie for
hours or even days, with their wounds undressed and
bleeding, exposed to the martial tramp of an infuriated
foe. Mournful is the loss of limbs. How we feel when
a neighbor by disease or accident, is compelled to submit
to a single amputation. How many subjects for amputation are furnished by a single victory ! How many, after
enduring the most excruciating sufferings, are maimed
and rendered helpless and miserable the remainder of
their days. Mournful is the loss of life, for where is the
human being who is not of importance to some one ?
How many a poor widow, whose name will never be announced in the public papers, is now weeping over a husband she will see no more ! How many an orphan is
now crying " My father ! O my father !" but that father
sleeps on the gory field of death, and will never again
caress the loved ones he has left behind. O, how many
fathers are this day saying, " Would God I had died for
thee, O my son !"

Mournful, above all, is the loss of souls ! We are far
from supposing that all warfare is unlawful, and that a
good man cannot be a soldier. Who has not read the
life of Colonel Gardiner, slain in battle at Prestonpans ?
Was there ever a mind more purely and ardently pious ?
A man may ascend to heaven from the field of battle, but
the moral state of our armies is too well known to be a
secret ! At any time the generality of those who com-
pose them are not prepared to die. How dreadfully affecting then, is it, to think of so many of our fellow
creatures being cut off in a moment, and sent with all
their sins upon them, to appear before the Judge of all ?
So many ways is victory turned into mourning.

Memorable in the annals of history will be the victory
at Gettysburg, Pennsylvania. Who can deny that its

unexampled suffering has spread a gloom over our whole country, and excited a deep and heartfelt sympathy for the unfortunate victims and their bereaved friends? By it, the hearts of many parents, brothers, sisters, companions and friends, have been filled with sadness. Religious, literary, and other associations have sustained a severe loss; and neighborhoods, towns, and the country at large, have been bereaved. The scenes of that event have made a thrilling appeal to the sympathies of this community.

They have shrouded in mourning a respected family in our midst, and to them cast a fearful pall over the joys of earth. They have removed forever from our sight an acquaintance and esteemed friend, whose early years were passed among us; who had often been a worshipper in this sanctuary; whose voice has often mingled with this choir, in the praise of God; one whose excellent qualities had secured for him the confidence and warm attachment of friends and relatives, and the respect of all who knew him.

Yes, among the thousands who fell upon that field of slaughter and death was Lieutenant-Colonel George Arrowsmith. By this afflictive and painful dispensation, not only have relatives been bereaved, but an extensive circle of acquaintances, who valued his friendship, enjoyed his society, respected his worth and entertained high expectations of his future usefulness, have been filled with unaffected sorrow. This affliction addresses itself to all who have been personal friends of the deceased. Strong are the ties of affection and friendship. From the stroke that sunders those ties, the heart recoils in untold agony. We hear of the death of an acquaintance and are sad. But when we know that a friend whom we loved and esteemed, and whose society and counsels we highly

prized, is no more, a tide of sorrow o'erflows our hearts;
but most of all, are we affected by being relatives of the
deceased. The common parent of mankind has estab-
lished the endearing relation of kindred, from which
spring the warmest, deepest and purest affections known
on earth. Others have their attachments, but not like
those who are bound together by the strong ties of con-
sanguinity. The distress occasioned to survivors by
the stroke of death is proportionate to the strength and
ardor of their affections! We, who are only acquaintances of the departed, are filled with sadness at the tidings of his melancholy fate, but of the sorrows of his afflicted and bereaved relatives, parents, brothers and sisters, we can have no adequate conception. The depths of
their hearts are stirred; the fountains of their sympathies
are broken up.

Among the most endearing relations of human life is
that of parent and child; their affections are reciprocal;
that of a parent, for wise purposes, is doubtless the
stronger. The child weeps at the loss of the parent, but
at the loss of the child the parent is filled with irrepressible and oftentimes inconsolable grief. The general in-
fanticide in Bethlehem, which occurred under the reign of
Herod, is symbolically represented by a paroxysm of maternal anguish; in Rama there was heard a loud lamenta-
tion and weeping and great mourning; when the patriarch
Jacob felt the sadness of such a bereavement, in vain did
his sons rise up to comfort him. He refused to be comforted and said, "I will go down to the grave to my son
in mourning." The poignancy of grief with which King
David mourned for an undutiful son, who died in an attempt against his father's life, we have already mentioned.
I will not mock the feelings of bereaved parents and relatives by attempting to give a description of their sor-

rows. Should I make the attempt, the most expressive
language I could employ, would do injustice to my
theme. These sorrows can be known only to the Omnipresent God, and the hearts that feel them.

Again the agreeableness of departed friends is another
circumstance which heightens the pain of bereavement.
One reason of David's distress at the death of his friend
Jonathan, is expressed in the words, "Very pleasant
hast thou been to me." Valuable and agreeable qualities
in our friends, endear them to our hearts and render
our separation more painful. Those who were acquainted
with the departed know him to have been a kind friend
and an agreeable associate; possessed of more than ordinary natural abilities, a highly cultivated mind united
with his practical good sense, acute discernment, sound
judgment, and Christian morality. These, like a beautiful constellation, shed their mild radiance around and
won for him the respect and love of a wide circle of
friends and acquaintances, who had indulged the hope
that his future might be honorable, happy and exten-
sively useful to his fellow men.

No more on the shores of time we shall meet our friend.
We have often met him and exchanged our cordial greet-
ings, we have loved his society, valued his friendship;
but never again shall we enjoy them here. For the last
time has he visited his native home! We sympathize
with the Elders and Christians at Ephesus, who wept
and fell on Paul's neck, sorrowing most of all for the
words which he spake unto them! That they should see
his face no more!

Lamented friend and brother, thine earthly race is
run. Thy mortal course is finished. Thy sun has fallen
before it reached its meridian altitude. Thy warfare is
accomplished. Thy tears are wiped away. Thou hast

entered that world where wars shall never come, and
" Where the wicked cease from troubling, and the weary
are at rest." We bid thee farewell! But thy memory
embalmed in the tears and affections of weeping kindred
and sorrowing friends shall still live.

To soothe the sorrows of this mournful event let us re-
flect: First—that it occurred under the immediate super-
vision of an All Wise Providence. Jehovah sits at the
helm of the universe, controlling all its vast affairs in
infinite wisdom and benevolence. He is able to bring
good out of evil. He causeth the wrath of man to praise
Him, and the remainder He restrains. He extends His
care and providence to the minutest particulars affecting
our interest. "Even the hairs of our head are all num-
bered," and "Not a sparrow falleth to the ground without His notice." Much less did this event occur without
His knowledge and permission. The human agency may
have been exceedingly culpable, as in the Saviour's cruci-
fixion, yet the Almighty Ruler of the world has ordained
it in His beneficence and love. We call this an untimely
death. True, it was death in the morning of life, yet it
is timely! The time and mode are of Divine selection.
The Great Shepherd of Israel, at the time and in the way
He sees fit, calls His sheep away from earthly storms and
tempests, to His glorious fold on high. Why should we
repine? He hath done all things well.

Second—Although we would neither eulogize the dead,
nor anticipate the decisions of the final day, yet may
we not cherish and express the humble hope that our
friend died a Christian? A subject of experimental and
practical Godliness? If so, his eulogy is written in the
word of God. "Blessed are the dead that die in the Lord
from hence forth. Yea, saith the Spirit, for they rest

from their labor, and their works do follow them." "Say
ye to the righteous, it shall be well with him."

For twenty-six days has his ransomed spirit been an
associate of angels, and the "Spirits of the just made
perfect," in rendering ascriptions of praise to our incar-
nate, yet Crucified Redeemer, in far more exalted strains
than mortals ever knew; while the unspeakable glories
of the heavenly world have been unfolding to his enrap-
tured vision. How the laurels of earth wither to the eyes
of such a company! Could we hold intercourse with the
eternal world, a whisper from the spirit land would
say to us, "Weep not for me." "The Saviour has passed
through the portals before me, and the lamp of His love
was my guide through the gloom."

Third—It shows us the supreme value of religion. How
plainly are we taught the vanity of all earthly good!
How loudly admonished to seek a heavenly treasure!
Nay, were the sea one crysolite, the earth one golden
ball, and diamonds all the stars of night, religion is
worth them all. In loudest accents this Providence
warns us to be in constant readiness to meet death. It
is a direct appeal to all who are unfurnished and unpre-
pared for the coming world. With strong emphasis, it
rebukes the spirit of procrastination, by which some
would put off the concerns of the soul. To the afflicted
family I would say, tender and endearing were the relations you sustained to the deceased. You had given him
a large place in the affections of your hearts. He was
worth all that you bestowed upon him. By his sudden
and appalling death you are filled with grief and mourning. To feel the ties of nature sundered, is painful in the
extreme. Your happy circle is broken. Your ranks are
invaded, and some of you feel that earth is stripped of
its joy. In your present affliction, receive our sympathies.

We mingle our tears with yours. The great Physician can heal your broken bones and bind up your bleeding hearts. To Him we commend you. Let faith lift her eye to the resurrection of the just, where you may be enabled to say to the Master, " Here am I, and the children which Thou hast given me." God grant you resignation to His holy will.

NOTE B.

HAMILTON VOLUNTEER AID ASSOCIATION, CORRESPONDENCE OF "THE REPUBLICAN."

The ladies of Hamilton met on Friday evening, May 31st, at the house of Mr. Adon Smith, to form themselves into an organization for the purpose of providing comforts for the volunteers sent from Hamilton and adjoining towns to fight for the Stars and Stripes. The notice not having been generally extended, the number present was not as large as desirable, but those present were earnest to be at work. Mrs. M. S. Platt was made chairman and the society organized under the name of the "Hamilton Volunteer Aid Association." Mrs. Charles Mason was unanimously elected president; Mrs. A. M. Beebe, vice-president; Miss Annette Foote, treasurer; and Miss D. W. Waters, secretary. It was resolved, after a discussion of the needs of the soldiers, to appropriate the funds first collected to the procuring of havelocks for Company D. It was further resolved, that the ladies of adjoining towns be invited to join the association and coöperate with the ladies of Hamilton. The following officers were then chosen : As soliciting committee, Mrs. G. W. Eaton, Mrs. Lewis Wickwire ; for havelocks, Mrs. Bancroft, Miss Mary Manchester, Mrs. Wells

Russell ; for sponge cases and towels, Mrs. John J. Foote, Mrs. M. Harmon ; for sewing kits, Miss M. A. Hastings, Miss V. M. Case ; for miscellaneous articles, Mrs. Frank Bonney, Miss C. Hyde. Mrs. Mason then read some proceedings of the Chenango Volunteer Association, and an interesting letter from Captain Arrowsmith, acknowledging the receipt of the provisions and clothing lately sent the volunteers. Mr. Miner kindly offered his parlors as a place of meeting, and the association adjourned to meet at the Wickwire House on Thursday, June 6th, at two o'clock, P. M., for the purpose of working for the volunteers, and making plans for future operations.

NOTE C.

WAR DEPARTMENT, WASHINGTON, August 19th, 1862.

Sir:

You are hereby informed that the President of the United States has appointed you Assistant Adjutant-General of Volunteers, with the rank of Captain, in the service of the United States, to rank as such from the nineteenth day of August, one thousand eight hundred and sixty-two. Should the Senate, at their next session, advise and consent thereto, you will be commissioned accordingly.

Immediately on receipt hereof, please to communicate to this Department, through the Adjutant-General's office, your acceptance or non-acceptance of said appointment ; and, with your letter of acceptance, return to the Adjutant-General of the Army the oath herewith enclosed, properly filled up, subscribed and attested, reporting at the same time your age, residence when appointed, and the state in which you were born.

Should you accept, you will at once report, in person, for orders, to Brigadier-General Z. B. Tower, U. S. Volunteers.

EDWIN M. STANTON,

Secretary of War.

CAPTAIN GEORGE ARROWSMITH,
Asst. Adjt. Genl. Vols.

NOTE D.

Extract from a letter of Hon. Charles Mason, L. L. D., of the Supreme Court of New York, to Thomas Arrowsmith, Esq., dated December 30th, 1863.

"You will pardon me in saying that the death of your son George was to me and my family the severest casualty of this terrible war. He was possessed of a noble and generous spirit, brave in danger, cool and composed in the midst of battle. He held most unbounded control over his men. This was so whether in camp or field, he always possessed their confidence and esteem. He was a remarkably good judge of human nature for one so young as he was, and would assuredly have acquired distinction in his chosen profession had he not gone into the army. I remonstrated against his going at the time he first enlisted, but he said he was already pledged to lead the company then in process of formation and he *could not back down.*

"I was one who went to Albany and presented to Governor Morgan an application for his appointment as Lieutenant-Colonel. The high commendation he received from officers of the army with whom he was associated in battle, as to his ability and military capacity to command either a regiment or brigade, induced the Governor to appoint him over other meritorious applicants for the position. He should have been appointed the Colonel, and so Governor Morgan said, but George was in the field and the regiment was half filled, and they must have a Colonel then."

NOTE E.

This conversation was told to the writer by Surgeon H. C. Hendrick of McGrawville, New York.

NOTE F.

These incidents were related to the writer by Captain G. T. VanHoesen of Cortland, New York, who served in the One Hundred and Fifty-seventh Regiment, New York State Volunteers, at Gettysburg.

NOTE G.

These figures are from official reports. and include a loss sustained by the remnant of the regiment in a fight on Culp's Hill, the evening of the second day's battle at Gettysburg.

NOTE H.

MEETING OF THE BRIGADE BOARD, FROM THE "MONMOUTH DEMOCRAT."

The Brigade Board of the Monmouth and Ocean Brigade met at the court-house in Freehold on Monday last at ten o'clock, A. M., and was called to order by General Haight.

Present, Brigadier-General Haight, Lieutenant-Colonel Green, Major Corlies, Major Green, Major Yard, Captain Forman, Captain Conover, Captain Hyer.

Captain Forman desired to call the attention of the

Board to the death of Lieutenant-Colonel George Arrow-smith, of the One Hundred and Fifty-seventh New York Volunteers, a native of this county and a son of Major Thomas Arrowsmith, who was killed while gallantly leading his regiment on the outskirts of the town of Gettysburg during the recent battle at that place. Captain Forman pronounced a high eulogy on the character of Lieutenant-Colonel Arrowsmith. He said there are few who leave a nobler record. While acting as Assistant Adjutant-General at Second Bull Run his name was brought permanently before the country. He deemed it proper for the Board to take some action in the matter expressive of their sentiments and to perpetuate the memory of the gallant dead.

Major Corlies moved that a committee of three be appointed to draft resolutions expressive of the sentiment of the board, relative to the death of Lieutenant-Colonel Arrowsmith, which was adopted, and General Haight, Major Conover and Captain Forman were appointed said committee.

The following resolutions in relation to the death of the above-named gallant young officer were reported by the committee and adopted :

WHEREAS, The Brigade Board of the Monmouth and Ocean Brigade, New Jersey Militia, have learned with deep regret that Lieutenant-Colonel George Arrow-smith, of the One Hundred and Fifty-seventh New York Volunteers, was killed while gallantly leading his regiment in the sanguinary conflict at Gettysburg on the third of July, in his efforts to expel the rebel armed force from the soil of Pennsylvania, and in defense of constitutional liberty; therefore,

Resolved, That we bow with contrite hearts to this dis-

position of an overruling Providence, who in this sad affliction has again sent a solemn admonition to warn us
that in the midst of life we are in death;

Resolved, That we recognize in the short and brilliant
career of Colonel Arrowsmith his patriotic endeavors to
restore to its wonted peace and unity our distracted and
unhappy country. Second Bull Run testifies to his activity in movement—his vigilance and reliability in danger ; Chancellorsville furnishes the indisputable evidence
of the living purpose that directed his movements, and
the unconquerable spirit that enabled him to undergo
the hardships and fatigues of battle; while Gettysburg
proves unflinching courage and determined bravery,
from the active part he took in the drama enacted there.

Resolved, That in the death we are called upon to
mourn, the military arm of the country has lost the services of a brave and accomplished officer, the cause of
constitutional government a bold and determined defend-
er, one who was willing to shed his blood in its defense;

Resolved, That this Board deeply sympathize with the
aged and esteemed parents and afflicted family of the deceased in their bereavement, and as an evidence of respect for the memory of the noble dead, this Board will
attend his funeral in the Baptist church in the village of
Middletown on Sunday, the nineteenth inst., at three
P. M.

Resolved, That copies of these resolutions be sent to the
family of the deceased and published in the county
papers.   Signed,

                              CHARLES HAIGHT,
                              FRANCIS CORLIES,
                              WILLIAM B. FORMAN,
                                   Committee.

NOTE I.

THE LATE LIEUTENANT-COLONEL ARROWSMITH.

The class of '59 of Madison University met at Hamilton, New York, the day and date hereafter given, and had its first reunion while attending the commencement of its Alma Mater, at which time the following preamble and resolutions were unanimously adopted :

WHEREAS, our beloved classmate, George Arrowsmith, Lieutenant-Colonel of the One Hundred and Fifty-seventh, New York State Volunteers, fell at Gettysburg July 3d, 1863, while nobly leading his regiment against the enemy; and

WHEREAS, the occasion of our first class reunion affords us the first opportunity of expressing our estimate alike of himself and of his early and noble fate; therefore

Resolved, That as a class we feel ourselves to have been peculiarly honored by the voluntary offering upon the nation's altar of a life so precious and valuable. While we miss him to-day, not as we do others, who, though absent, still live and work on earth, but as one we shall see here no more, we yet experience a mournful pleasure in transferring his name from the list of living classmates to that immortal scroll on which are inscribed the names of those who have laid down their lives for Liberty, God and their country;

Resolved, That in the sacrifice of his life, our class has lost one who united with distinguished originality of mind, a heart generous in its impulses, tenacious in its friendships and courageous in its instincts, all which invested him with the surest promises of success in whatever profession of life he might have chosen;

Resolved, That while we embalm his memory in our hearts' most sacred place, deeply conscious of our irreparable loss, we yet regard his identification with the cause of the nation in its second great struggle for nationality, and his subsequent death, as acts performed in our behalf, and we embrace this occasion to reässert our devotion to our country, and bind ourselves more closely upon the altar whereon his fresh young manhood was so heroically sacrificed, assured that he died not in vain, and that all familiar with his career must be stimulated to like noble endeavors;

Resolved, That in this first sundering of the golden chain of our class relations we are not unmindful of the desolation which has fallen upon his endeared home and parents, and that we hereby avail ourselves of the first opportunity given us as a class to tender the bereaved home circle of our lamented classmate our profound and heartfelt sympathy in this painful and sad bereavement;

Resolved, That a copy of these resolutions be given to the parents of the deceased, and that the same be published in the Hamilton *Republican*, the Utica *Morning Herald*, and the New Jersey *Standard*.

> GEORGE M. STONE,
> ENOS CLARKE,
> *Committee on Resolutions.*

Hamilton, August 17th, 1863.

Errata.

Page 96, line 6 from bottom, for "base" read bass.

Page 121, line 6, for "1862" read 1863. This letter and the letter that follows, should come after letter of December 30, 1862, on page 187.

Page 251, line 11, for "permanently" read prominently.

www.ingramcontent.com/pod-product-compliance
Lightning Source LLC
Chambersburg PA
CBHW020352030726
47496CB00007B/2108